THE
DEADLY
GLADIATRIX

Under the reign of Emperor Hadrian (117—138 A.D.), the power of the Roman Empire reaches to the borders of the known world, and even the most remote provinces enjoy unprecedented peace and prosperity.

On the well-fortified northern border of the empire, the Limes, lies the future metropolis of Vienna—Vindobona— at this point no more than a legionary camp, flanked by two insignificant civilian settlements.

Gladiator games are one of the most popular spectacles in the whole of the empire. However, the bloodshed should be limited to the arena...

I

The second day of the games dawned with bright sunshine and unusual warmth, at least for a day in March in the otherwise fairly harsh climate of Vindobona. Our small amphitheater was packed. Young and old were eagerly awaiting the continuation of a spectacle that had opened brilliantly yesterday, and which held out the prospect of further highlights today.

When I speak of games in this case, of course I do not mean the athletic contests so popular among the Greeks, but that bloody type of entertainment favored by the Romans.

Gladiator fights: a ritual that had originally been introduced to honor the dead, but which in recent centuries had evolved into a spectacle quite unique in our world. Not even amongst the diverse peoples that the Romans group together under the name of Germanic tribes—and to which I also belong—do we know such bloodthirstiness solely for the amusement of the masses. Of course, we do sometimes sacrifice some unfortunate prisoner of war in honor of the gods, and we are also no strangers to public executions raised to the level of a spectacle. But I digress....

Last fall, just as I had returned from my trip to the Wonders of the World, which I've recounted in my last chronicle, a man named Varro opened Vindobona's first gladiatorial school.

We could not, of course, compare ourselves with Carnuntum, the capital of our province, but over the years Vindobona had nevertheless grown to a population of thirty to thirty-five thousand, including the legion stationed here, and the good citizens did not get to enjoy great gladiatorial games nearly often enough.

Varro must have thought along those lines, or something similar, when he decided to establish his *ludus*—his gladiator school—here, of all places, in this remote corner of the empire. The man was probably deeply attached to his homeland, on which he had turned his back for many years. Now, in his old age, he had so much money at his disposal that the economic success of his venture was of secondary importance to him. It was why he'd settled the ludus in Vindobona and not in a more suitable place, I suppose.

It was said in the forum, in taverns, and wherever else gossip flourished, that Varro had sold himself to the gladiator school of Carnuntum in his youth owing to a huge mountain of debt. There he'd started an impressive career as a spear fighter, eventually managed to buy his way out, and then traveled the empire as a free gladiator. During a performance in Londinium he'd met a fabulously rich widow who had lost her heart to him.

However, one should not think that Varro was a good-looking specimen. As far as I—a man—could judge, he really didn't look like the classic hero, with his rather small stature, extremely broad but sloping shoulders and pronounced bow legs. His dark hair was also beginning to thin out, for which he tried to compensate with copious amounts of pomade. He would stand out among a crown of people as the one whose skull shone the most conspicuously.

For women, however, the strong, death-defying gladiators were among the most desirable of men—despite or perhaps because of their bad reputation, and regardless of whether they were physically attractive, or looked like the good Varro. It was the masculinity that mattered, the courage, and their overconfident, not to say arrogant, demeanor. Some fighters were virtually idolized by female admirers. The seemingly unequal marriage between Varro and the wealthy widow was therefore not surprising; after all, it was not an isolated case.

Varro finally retired from active combat and returned with his new wife to his beloved home city, Vindobona, where the poor woman was soon stricken down by an insidious disease.

Varro prepared a luxurious funeral for her and told everyone who wanted to hear it, and everyone else too, how much he had loved his wife and how hard her loss had hit him. In the end, however, he consoled himself by using his inherited fortune to found Vindobona's new gladiator school.

He seemed to have set his mind on outshining the old-established school of Carnuntum with this new ludus. That school was after all famous for its fighters, and far beyond the borders of the province.

Our town's wealthy citizens were quite taken with Varro's ambitious undertaking, and three of them had taken it upon themselves to host, in other words to finance, the first big games in Vindobona with fighters from the new school. This was a great honor for these citizens; it increased both their popularity among the people and the prestige of their families. The fact that it also emptied their coffers played only a minor role.

The games were to be staged over five days, and the main sponsor of the spectaculum was none other than my good friend Marcellus.

Marcellus ... need I introduce him any further? He is well known to faithful readers of my chronicles.

He was the legate, that is, the commander-in-chief of the legionary camp of Vindobona. Although he came from a noble Roman family and was still a very young man—unlike me—we got along splendidly. Which was astonishing, considering the fact that at the beginning of our acquaintance he had accused me of murder and then shortly afterwards stolen Layla, my lover, from me. You see, I am not a petty man and certainly not a barbarian, as ignorant Romans like to call us Germanics.

But back to the gladiatorial games. Besides Marcellus, two other honorable—and very wealthy—citizens of Vindobona had distinguished themselves as sponsors of the games.

Cornix was a merchant like me, but of Celtic descent. Unlike me, he maintained business relations exclusively with Rome and the central provinces of the empire, while I—with all modesty—can boast of being active even in the remotest regions of the empire, and beyond.

I can certainly claim to be a wealthy man, but Cornix was stinking rich, you had to give him that. Apparently he was a better businessman than I, but after all he was already running his trading empire in the third generation, whereas I'd had to build up everything myself.

Cornix was now approaching fifty years of age, yet he still had the figure and vitality of a youth. His slightly reddish hair was thick, with only a few gray strands, and so was his beard. Cornix always knew how to dress after the latest fashion, and was also a witty and cultured conversationalist.

The second co-sponsor of the games besides Cornix was Aurelius Iulianus, a Roman citizen and member of the council of our city. His fortune had come from an unusual source, for Iulianus was a dentist. Not a very prestigious business, but the dentures he knew how to make were the best between Vindobona and Rome. At least that was what he claimed, and therefore he managed to collect imperial prices for his workpieces.

A typical upstart; the new rich. Iulianus and his wife enjoyed throwing their money around, but at least they did a lot of good for our city and its inhabitants in the process.

As far as his character was concerned, Iulianus was rather pompous, and humor seemed to be an unknown concept to him. Physically he was skinny, probably ten years younger than Cornix, but his face already showed deep wrinkles, as though life had given him a hard time. His hair was pitch black—he must dye it with that disgusting colorant made from decaying leeches, the name of which I always tended to forget.

These two men were now sitting side by side with Marcellus at the very front of the arena's VIP stand. In the second row, next to me, two women had taken their seats. To my left sat Petronella, the wife of Iulianus, a Roman matron with quite a full body. Her blonde—or rather bleached—hair was piled up in a complicated hairstyle, her neck and arms heavily adorned with jewelry, and there was a highly critical expression on her face at all times. It was as if nothing could ever be good enough for her.

On my right sat Layla, who was Marcellus's mistress, as I have already mentioned. If she had not been a former slave, he probably would have married her long ago. Unfortunately such a marriage was unthinkable for the scion of a noble Roman family.

Layla came from the kingdom of Nubia, deep within Africa. Her skin and hair were the color of ebony, and she could rightly be called an extraordinary beauty. But even more impressive were Layla's mental powers: I recall that in most of the murder cases we had already been involved with together, she had been the one to solve everything in the end.

I had once loved Layla very much, and had done everything I could to win her back after Marcellus got in my way. I had even invited her on a trip around the world—where we'd again had to deal with a series of murders. At the end of the trip, we had come to the conclusion that the gods had chosen us to be murder investigators, and we'd decided to actively offer this service to people who needed it.

During the trip around the world I had also met a Roman widow named Alma. Or rather a blond Northerner who had been *married* to a Roman. Over the corpses we'd encountered during our world trip we had actually become closer, as morbid as that may sound, and Alma had subsequently been my guest in Vindobona. Over the winter she'd returned to Rome, but now another of her visits was pending. She was a little reluctant, it seemed to me, to make another commitment. Her husband had been a real tyrant, and now she wanted to enjoy the freedom she'd regained a little. And yet she was fond of me, or at least, that was my impression.

I awaited Alma's arrival in Vindobona any day now, even though I must admit that the games pleasantly mitigated my impatience. Perhaps she would arrive in time to witness the last day or two of the spectacle.

Today's program would follow the usual tradition, as it had already done yesterday. In the morning, animal rushes and the fights of the so-called *venatores* against dangerous beasts were scheduled. Then at noon, the executions of criminals would follow, and finally in the afternoon, as a highlight, the actual gladiator fights would commence.

For the procurement of the animals I had recommended my friend Faustinius. I had known him for ages, but had lost sight of him and then met him again on the aforementioned trip around the world the previous year. When I'd heard about the new gladiator school and the first planned games after my return to Vindobona, I had gone to Varro, the *lanista*—that is, the principal—and had suggested the services of Faustinius to him.

And my old friend had not disappointed us; he had arrived barely a week before the start of the games with his luxurious travel wagons and small army of slaves and delivered almost a hundred exquisite beasts to Varro. From the more familiar wolves and bears to lions and leopards from Africa, tigers from faraway Asia, as well as huge snakes, bulls and deer.

A bull and a bear, which had been tied together with a long chain, had just been brought into the arena. The people were already in high spirits, despite the early hour, and cheered the two opponents with fervent shouts. From what I could understand from the earsplitting bawling, the bear was the favorite of this duel.

I was not so sure. The bull was a magnificent specimen, and anyone who might get acquainted with his horns would probably not live long enough to make another counterattack, no matter the sharp claws and teeth with which he might be armed.

The bear probably saw it in a similar way. He straightened up on his hind legs, eager to fight and with a wild roar, but kept the maximum possible distance from the bull that was allowed by the chain.

I was to miss what happened next, because just at that moment I heard a familiar voice behind me.

"Sorry to bother you, Thanar."

II

I turned my head in surprise and looked right into the worried eyes of Optimus. He was a veteran of the army, who had retired from Marcellus's legion some time ago.

He had accompanied Layla and me as leader of the guard on our world tour, and we had become friends. Optimus was a loyal fellow and a very capable fighter, with a brave heart and a keen sense of humor.

After our return home, I had offered him the post of my chief guard—after all, I sometimes traded in very valuable goods that needed protection on my long transport routes.

But Varro, the lanista, with his newly founded gladiator school, had gotten in my way. Optimus had turned out to be an ardent supporter of gladiatorial games and had preferred to enter Varro's service as chief guard instead of starting with me.

I did not hold it against him; I think everyone should pursue the work that fills him with the greatest joy.

So Optimus now presided over the guards of the gladiator school, and made sure that none of the enslaved fighters tried to escape, or seize the weapons to which the gladiators otherwise only had access during the fights in the arena.

A gladiator was a dangerous man—several dozen of them, like those in Varro's school, could gather into a gang of murderers and quickly incite a slave revolt in the province.

The uprising of long ago, which had been led by an escaped gladiator named Spartacus, yet remained horribly fresh in the people's memory. Entire legions had been bloodily beaten by these rebels.

Well, with my friend Optimus in charge, the safety of Varro's gladiator school was in the best hands. I had no doubt about that.

I was all the more surprised when he now leaned down to me with a worried face and reported to me in an excited whisper. Something seemed to have thrown the veteran of the legion out of his otherwise stoic calm. An expression of perplexity clouded his forehead.

Layla, always possessed of inexhaustible curiosity, turned away from the action in the arena and toward Optimus as well.

"Something strange has happened," Optimus began. "There at the ludus. In Varro's school."

He didn't wait for a reaction from either of us, but immediately continued: "Yesterday afternoon—the fight between Mevia the murmillo and the gladiatrix here in the arena—you watched it, didn't you?"

I nodded. Mevia was a rather inexperienced gladiator, an *ad gladium* convict, which meant that he had been condemned to serve in the gladiator school as punishment for some capital crime, probably murder. Every fight he survived extended his time on earth, but in the end, within two years at the latest, he would inevitably be executed provided no opponent had finished him off by then.

Among the gladiators there were so many different types—depending on armament, permitted armor and fighting style. Mevia fought as a *murmillo*, a heavy swords-man with a large shield and helmet. Murmillones were slow and sometimes heavy-footed, but well protected against the blows of their enemies.

His opponent yesterday afternoon had been Nemesis—a female gladiatrix! Yes, there really was such a thing, even if it was considered a rarity.

Nemesis had chosen the name of the goddess of venge-ance for herself, and it suited her perfectly. She was a fiery, dark-haired Amazon and skilled in martial arts that were out of this world.

Usually, female gladiators were pitted against other women, or occasionally against more comedic fighters, dwarfs, for example. But Nemesis took on quite ordi-nary—no, even excellent—male opponents.

She fought wearing light armor, wielding a small round shield and a curved sword—which was her talisman.

Supposedly, it had been forged many centuries ago for a legendary queen of the Amazons. The gladiatrix had never spoken a word about how it had come into her possession.

It was rumored that Nemesis was originally the daughter of a most reputable family. Some even claimed that her father was a senator.

It sometimes happened that rebellious offspring of re-spectable families turned their backs on their own kindred and sought adventure. Some enrolled in gladiatorial schools, seeking the ultimate challenge, glory, mortal dan-ger, and the passionate adoration of the masses.

In truth, however, little was known about this mysteri-ous gladiatrix, apart from the fact that she had already been celebrating glorious triumphs in various arenas of the empire for several years.

In any case, Nemesis seemed to be a favorite of the gods.

Their fight had been an unequal one from the beginning; the murmillo had fought with the determination of the doomed man that he was, but he'd ultimately stood no chance against Nemesis.

In the end, Marcellus had at least spared his life this time—at the request of the audience—because Mevia had proven himself brave and delivered an exciting spectacle. The audience loved that kind of a show, and the sponsors of the games usually bowed to their wishes when deciding the life or death of a gladiator.

"Mevia only came out of the fight slightly injured, remember?" Optimus whispered to me.

I nodded. "Yes, he survived once again. He was able to extend his sad life for a few more weeks or months. Until the next battle—or his final execution."

Optimus shook his head. "That's exactly what I had thought. But Mevia passed away last night. Atticus, our medic at the school, can't explain it."

He gave me a worried look. "That's why I've come to you. I think something's wrong with the manner of Mevia's death."

"What are you trying to say?" interjected Layla. "That he was murdered? Are there any signs of that on his body?"

As always, she remained matter-of-fact, even appearing curious, where other women would have long since turned away with a shudder. Death, even violent ones, instilled neither revulsion nor fear in her.

Optimus twisted the corners of his mouth. "Mevia suffered a few superficial cuts in the fight. Atticus tended to them; the man got his dinner, and then he was locked up again in his cell. It's where we found him dead this morning. No one had access to Mevia after the fight except for me and my men, the guards of the school. And Atticus ... well, he suspects that Mevia was poisoned as early as yesterday. With a substance that didn't immediately unfold its murderous effect, if you know what I mean."

"Who would want to murder a man condemned *ad gladium*?" objected Layla. "He's doomed to die anyway, sooner or later."

"That's just it," Optimus said. "Only one person had a motive to poison Mevia—to weaken him for the fight. His eventual death may not have been intentional at all."

"You mean Nemesis?" I asked.

Optimus nodded. "Personally, I don't think she had anything to do with it," he said emphatically. "But Atticus suspects her. Maybe she's not as indomitable an Amazon as she pretends to be, he thinks. Maybe she's cheating, using poison to gain an advantage in battle. Or she's working some kind of deadly magic."

He shook his head. "I don't want to believe it. But I also can't think of any other explanation for Mevia's sudden death; that's why I'm here. Can you help me, Thanar? Take a look at the matter?"

He gave Layla an uncertain sideways glance.

"And you too, of course, if you want," he added.

He knew, as I did, that Layla was an outstanding investigator—as unusual as that might seem in a woman.

"A woman who can defeat men in battle," Layla murmured, "and immediately you think she must be a cheat. That she must resort to poison or foul magic to achieve her victories." She screwed up her face.

Nemesis seemed to fascinate Layla.

Well, it didn't surprise me; the gladiatrix was a strong, independent and very stubborn woman. Much like Layla, too.

I promised Optimus that we would meet at Varro's ludus that evening after the games to get to the bottom of Mevia's sudden death.

III

I'd completely lost my focus. Long after Optimus had disappeared again, my thoughts were still circling around the strange death of Mevia, and I hardly took any notice of the spectaculum unfolding in the arena.

Was the gladiatrix really too good to be true? A skilled deceiver who weakened her opponents with poison before the fight, so that she could seemingly defeat them in triumph?

The longer I thought about it, the more I came to the conclusion that Mevia's fight against Nemesis yesterday had indeed ... how should I put it? That he had seemed to be somehow impaired. Yes, that was the best way to describe it.

He had fought like a wild animal, yet had somehow seemed uncoordinated and a bit clumsy. Yesterday I had attributed this to the fact that he was still a rather inexperienced fighter, but in truth there might have been something much more insidious behind his behavior: a poison that had numbed his senses and diminished his fighting ability.

And now Mevia was dead.

My gaze wandered back to the sands of the arena, where a very skilled *venator*, an animal fighter, was taking on two lions at once. The animals were magnificent to behold, and I knew from Faustinius that they had not been fed for several days.

In case their fighting spirit was still not great enough, some arena slaves were ready with whips and torches to incite the animals against the venator.

There was a rapt expression on the face of Petronella, the wife of Iulianus, who was sitting next to me. Her gaze, however, was not on the beasts, it seemed to me, but rather on the fighter, who was a very handsome fellow.

Petronella had clearly already passed forty, and her husband Iulianus, as I have already described, was not exactly a handsome man. So perhaps she found pleasure in looking at a strong and death-defying young fellow whose sweat-covered muscles were glistening in the sunlight.

It had turned into a hard fight, really worth seeing. Several times the venator went down; once, one of the lions started to sink his fangs into the man's neck, but the fighter did not only know how to use his sword as a weapon. He gave the lion such a violent broadside with his shield that it jumped away snarling.

Finally, the venator managed to kill one of the beasts. With a sword stroke worthy of Hercules, he struck down the mighty cat. Taking down the second was much easier, and finally the two majestic beasts lay dead in the sand. Their flesh would be served tonight as an exotic delicacy for upscale visitors of the games.

Executions were usually carried out at noon. Some guests left the arena at this time, preferring to enjoy a sumptuous lunch instead of the brutal spectacle. Others were particular lovers of this part of the program.

Among the latter was Marcellus. While the other two sponsors, Cornix and Iulianus, and Petronella withdrew, the legate remained in his seat, waiting anxiously for the spectacle. He had a slave bring refreshments for us, and then turned his full attention back to the arena, where an elaborate stage set was being erected at lightning speed. A landscape of rocks and tall grass in front of the columns of a Greek temple was recreated, and I began to ponder what deadly spectacle it would serve as a backdrop to.

Varro really had spared no expense and effort for these games. I did not even dare to calculate what the spectaculum must have cost Marcellus and his co-sponsors.

When criminals were executed in the course of gladiatorial games, they were often finished off in a rather conventional way; in small provincial arenas like ours, this was usually the case. The villains were beheaded, burned or strangled, or they were made to fight each other to the death. Often—and this was perhaps the most popular method of execution—they were also thrown to wild animals.

Unlike the venatores, the professional animal gladiators, the condemned criminals were not given a weapon, shield or armor when they faced the beasts in the arena. With bare fists, clad only in a loincloth, they had to take on their four-legged opponents.

In these duels, unlike in the venator fights, the beasts almost always emerged victorious.

In larger cities, or even in Rome itself, executions were often staged as great spectacles. Mythical battles were reenacted in which the condemned slaughtered each other. Or there were famous scenes that required fewer people.

The fall of Icarus from the sky, for example.

For this purpose, a scaffold would be erected in the arena, feathered wings were put on the condemned, and ... well, you can guess the rest, can't you? The wings never worked; every time, the condemned fell to his death.

Varro, the lanista and organizer of the games, had promised us some very special executions. I was curious.

Not only did I want to know what particular spectacle he had come up with—I was also a little proud of Layla and myself. Through our investigative work we ourselves had hunted down two of the criminals who were to meet their fate in the course of these games.

Layla and I had, as already mentioned, decided at the end of our world tour to deliberately turn to solving murder cases. We wanted to put the skills we had acquired in this field at the service of the general public.

We had agreed to call ourselves *detectores*, that is, investigators or sleuths. But as one can easily imagine, Marcellus was not very enthusiastic about his beloved's new endeavor. We should have foreseen this not-inconsiderable obstacle, but had somehow overlooked it in our zeal.

So we couldn't really advertise our services, or even have them called out in the forum. That had worried us at the beginning. But, as in the past, it turned out not to be necessary at all to actively search for suitable cases; the murders found us all by themselves. And the gods made sure that we had our hands full.

At the winter solstice, Layla and I had been on the trail of a poisoner who had sent her unloved husband to the afterlife with the help of a generous dose of belladonna. She was to meet her death in the arena tomorrow or the day after—in a reenactment of that mythical encounter between Pasiphae and the bull.

Some of my most esteemed and highly educated readers will be familiar with this story: Pasiphae was of divine birth, and married to Minos, the king of Crete. However, when the latter angered the gods by denying them a particularly magnificent bull as a sacrifice, the immortals set out to take revenge.

As is so often the case, this did not fall upon the culprit himself, but his wife. Layla, who always passionately stood up for the rights of her sex, was enraged by this ... but I don't want to digress.

To punish the king, the divine Poseidon made Pasiphae fall passionately in love with that very bull. He even brought the poor woman to the point that she wanted to unite intimately with the animal.

From this abominable act of love came the Minotaur, that legendary hybrid creature of bovine and man. Later, seven youths and seven maidens from Athens regularly had to be sacrificed to this monster in the Labyrinth deep beneath the royal palace.

Said union of Pasiphae with the bull should now serve as a template for the death penalty of the ruthless poisoner. I will refrain from a further description in order not to disturb the more squeamish among my readers.

The second criminal we had hunted down, only a few weeks ago, was a certain Brigantius, or at least that's what he called himself.

He could justifiably be considered a big fish that had only been caught with great effort and sometimes very dangerous personal commitment. Brigantius was the long-sought leader of a notorious band of robbers, who had been the true scourge of Vindobona's inhabitants as well as travelers on the surrounding roads.

People were not only divested of their belongings; they often even lost their lives in these encounters.

Today at noon, this Brigantius was to be punished with death in the arena. I was already most curious to see what fate the good Varro had devised for him. Such a dangerous, even notorious, villain had to meet a spectacular end—we were all agreed on that.

According to hints that Optimus had dropped to me, several of the tasks of the famous hero Hercules were to be re-enacted—with the small but subtle difference that Brigantius would not come out of the challenges alive.

I assumed that the bandit would have to fight a series of beasts in front of the appropriate backdrop for each. Hercules had defeated the Nemean Lion, the Erymanthian Boar, the Hydra....

Would one of the two giant snakes that Faustinius had delivered perhaps be used instead of the Hydra? Marcellus, Layla and I had already marveled at these monsters in their cages, and they had not been fed for a long time.

It was said that the monster snakes could put even a grown man in such a stranglehold with their thigh-thick bodies that his strongest bones would break.

IV

In view of these—admittedly very high—expectations, I was all the more surprised when we had to wait for the first execution of the day for an unusually long amount of time.

Then a prisoner unknown to me was led into the amphitheater and burned at the stake without much ado. The fellow was already making an impression of being half-dead when he was dragged into the arena. Had he been tortured so severely beforehand that he was now barely in his right mind? That would have been unusual, because after all the audience wanted to experience an active spectacle, to feast on the death throes of the victim.

This poor fellow was tied to the stake, cried out once briefly when the first flames licked at him, but then either quickly fainted or even breathed his last before he was completely engulfed by the fire.

The elaborate landscape that had been built was not involved in the action.

I honestly wasn't sad to have not witnessed an agonizing death. In truth, while I found the staging of ancient myths fascinating, I wasn't really fond of the executions themselves. Even if these criminals deserved to die for their bloody deeds, I felt no need to watch their punishments in person.

But the death of this man nevertheless seemed strange.

It was banal and had bored the spectators. No surprise, then, that the sensation-hungry people acknowledged this first execution of the day with numerous disapproving shouts.

The burning was followed by an excruciatingly long pause—then our poisoner was led into the arena. Her execution had definitely not been planned for today.

"Strange," I heard Layla mutter, and Marcellus also put on a displeased expression.

I whispered to the two of them that I wanted to take a look behind the scenes. I immediately left my seat and made my way into the hidden underground of the arena, where spectators normally had no business. But as a guest of honor of the main sponsor, I was not denied access.

In the corridor where the temporary dungeons of the condemned were located, I met Rusticus. He was one of the guard slaves of the gladiator school, under the command of my good Optimus. He was a lanky fellow, perhaps thirty years old, with black hair, a full beard, and a receding high forehead that made him look more educated than he probably was.

He seemed surprised to see me down here, and it didn't escape me how his eyes widened.

The fact that some of the other men from the ludus— guards, arena slaves and other personnel—were running around like startled chickens, shouting contradictory orders at each other and all seeming quite overwhelmed, only confirmed my impression. Something was very wrong here.

Many of the holding cells of the doomed were empty, although they should have been well filled for the midday program.

There was nothing to be seen of Varro, but one could probably not expect even the most zealous lanista to supervise every single process in the arena's underground himself.

"We can't carry out the executions as planned," Rusticus began to tell me. "We have to improvise because..."

He swallowed, rolling his eyes as if desperately searching for the right words. At the same time, he rummaged around in his beard with his dirty fingers.

He had to take a deep breath before he could continue. "We keep those who are to be executed at the ludus until they are brought to the arena, but something terrible has happened there. A curse has struck us!"

He gasped breathlessly, deeply agitated. His dark eyes were almost coming out of their sockets.

I asked him with a questioning look to give me more details.

"Just before we were about to transport the condemned from the ludus today, there—"

He faltered, looking even more frightened. "They all just died, sir. Before our eyes! As if they had been struck down by the hand of the gods. As if a demon raged among them ... and not only among the victims destined for today, but quite indiscriminately. Seven or eight of those to be executed were struck down. They were suddenly writhing on the ground in death spasms. And the fellow we just burned was also half gone when we brought him here!"

"I didn't miss that," I replied. "Nor did the rest of the audience, I'm afraid."

Rusticus ruffled his hair, "Oh, dear! But we couldn't do

anything about it, I swear! Atticus, our medicus, was right there when the dying began, of course. He was able to save one or two lives, but it was too late for the others. Because of this, we now have barely enough living villains for noon today, let alone the rest of the games. We've had to quickly reorganize the program. Do you think Marcellus and the other sponsors will forgive us? We can only offer a very limited spectacle as far as executions are concerned."

He seemed genuinely worried.

I made no reply. The angry shouts of the spectators, which by now sounded like veritable battle cries, could be heard even down here.

"What about Brigantius?" I asked him instead. "The robber chief who was supposed to die today? Don't tell me he was also among those who died at the ludus?"

Rusticus nodded sheepishly. "I'm afraid he was, sir. You yourself hunted him down so heroically, didn't you? Now he's dead as a doornail, and no one could enjoy his passing."

I was unreceptive to his attempt at flattery, although of course Rusticus was not to blame that the robber had now escaped his just punishment, having met such an unspectacular end away from the hungry audience.

I could get over it. As I've said, I was not a great lover of the execution spectacles.

But what Rusticus had told me, that seven or eight of those to be put to death had met an untimely end in the gladiator school, caused me great concern. If one added the sudden death of the gladiator Mevia, which Optimus had reported to me only a few hours ago, then something was not right at all in the ludus.

I really had to pay a visit to the gladiator school, but now there was not enough time for it. And in the afternoon—now that the audience had become so enraged—I had better not leave the VIP stand. That would have been a slap in the face to my friend Marcellus and the other sponsors.

So I returned to my seat, but I had neither eyes nor ears for the executions that were yet to come. There were only a few, owing to the lack of living people to bring into the arena.

The gaps in the program were half filled with dancers, musicians and jokers, who usually offered diversion for the noontime interlude, between the carrying out of the death sentences. These men and women did their best, extending the times of their performances somewhat, and managed to appease the demanding audience a little.

V

The afternoon gladiator fights succeeded in capturing my attention again, at least to a certain extent. I was looking forward to the last two fights of the day with particular excitement.

The first of the two duels was to be fought between very different opponents, but that was precisely what made the gladiator games so attractive. Good and unusual pairings were the be-all and end-all of the arena. The audience loved the new, the exotic, things they hadn't already seen a dozen times.

One fighter was a veteran of the games, a Nordic-style axeman named Telephus, who had been a real crowd favorite for many years.

Even the name promised an extraordinary hero: Telephus, the far shining, son of Hercules....

The gladiators or their owners rarely showed excessive modesty when it came to choosing names.

Varro had bought Telephus—an unfree fighter who still had two or three years to serve—from the gladiator school at Carnuntum. For the sum rumored to have changed hands in the process, one could have afforded a nice little townhouse in Vindobona. But good gladiators were worth the investment; it was a credit to the sponsors of the games if they could boast such celebrities.

Telephus's opponent today was not yet a well-known

fighter, but his star had risen very steeply into the gladiatorial sky in the last year or two. An insider tip, one might say, who until now had only been known to connoisseurs. But that might change today, if he managed to defeat a veteran like Telephus.

The fighter's name was Hilarius, which meant 'cheerful.' A somewhat unfortunate choice, in my humble opinion. It sounded neither particularly glorious nor fearsome. But perhaps the man meant it to express his optimism that he would see the end of his career—no small feat for a gladiator.

Hilarius was hardly older than twenty and thus about ten years younger than his opponent. Moreover, he was a very handsome fellow, of tall stature and athletic build. Slim and agile—and an instant favorite of the female audience.

When he entered the arena, he was greeted by joyful jeers and passionate gestures from the women. Kisses were blown to him, and less respectable representatives of the female sex—at the top of the ranks—shouted ambiguous invitations to the handsome gladiator. Or should I say, unambiguous ones.

Layla, sitting next to me, grinned with amusement. Petronella, on my other side, shook her head indignantly.

Hilarius was a *retiarius*—one of the most popular types of gladiator. Such a fighter had no armor apart from a shield-like padding on his left arm, and his weaponry was more reminiscent of a fisherman than a warrior. He fought with a long trident and a throwing net, with which he aimed to catch his opponents, or at least try to restrict their freedom of movement.

Hilarius embodied this gladiator-type excellently. While

Telephus, with his armor, helmet, shield, and heavy axe, had to rely on strength rather than agility, the retiarius was light on his feet. He pranced around his opponent, repeatedly trying to land a deft throw with the net—only to pick it up again from the sand after a failed attempt, risking his life in doing so.

The trident as a weapon gave him greater reach, but when Telephus moved to attack with axe and shield, only the young man's agility stood between him and certain death.

In the bets that were being placed with great passion—albeit illegally—on the gladiator fights, Telephus was considered the favorite. At least, as far as I had noticed.

I myself was not a gambler, and did not bet my money on one or other outcome of the duels. I simply enjoyed the spectacle, perfect in terms of combat, skill and the courage of the gladiators.

The fight dragged on for quite a long time, Hilarius attacking courageously again and again. Telephus, however, behaved like a turtle. He remained on the defensive, seemingly intent on tiring out his opponent.

Of course, this was not a bad strategy to bring a retiarius to his knees—after all, he depended on his speed and agility. But it was not what the public desired. The audience wanted to see daring, foolhardiness and the defiance of death in a fighter, not a tame spectacle that offered few thrills.

I had not seen Telephus fight anywhere in the neighboring provincial arenas on any previous occasion. But I didn't understand how he could have gained such popularity when he fought like a coward.

In the end, however, the veteran's strategy panned out. Hilarius had used up too much of his strength in his spirited attacks; he became careless and finally went down after Telephus gave him a spectacular broadside with his shield.

Hunched over, but without uttering a sound of pain, Hilarius now lay at the feet of his opponent. He humbly raised the usual two fingers in the air to ask the audience for *missio*.

Missio—this meant the same as a pardon. If the spectators granted it, Hilarius was allowed to leave the arena alive. If not, he had to offer his neck to Telephus, who would quickly put an end to him with his axe.

The majority of the audience opted for the cut-throat gesture that demanded a death sentence, while bawling loudly. The fight had not pleased them, although that was clearly due to Telephus and not Hilarius himself. Besides, some of the more bloodthirsty spectators were probably still disgruntled because of the half-hearted executions at noon. They wanted to see blood.

Marcellus looked toward Cornix and Iulianus, his two co-sponsors. Both men leaned over and whispered something to him, first Cornix, then the dentist. The latter placed one of his bony hands on the legate's arm and clearly came too close to him. I didn't like this gesture of ingratiation—from the new rich to the scion of old nobility. But Marcellus seemingly took no offence.

I couldn't hear what the two men were saying to my friend, although I tried hard to pick up a few words at least. Layla wasn't the only one with a fair amount of curiosity, I have to admit.

Marcellus listened to the two wordlessly and kept a straight face. Finally, he stood up.

The roar of the crowd died down a bit. Many heads now turned expectantly away from the two fighters in the arena and toward the legate. What would Marcellus decide?

"Hilarius fought bravely," he announced in a raised voice. "I want to see him in more battles. Therefore, missio!"

He raised his index and middle fingers, as Hilarius had done, and extended them to the people in a commanding gesture.

He received some cheers, but at least as much indignation. Telephus obeyed him without hesitation: he let go of the defeated, even helping Hilarius to stand on his feet. The two gladiators walked out of the arena exhausted, but alive. Their careers would not end here and now.

Hilarius leaned on the elder as on a loyal friend. He was limping badly, but did not miss the opportunity to leave the battleground with his head held high.

VI

When crier and trumpets announced the last fight of the day, the audience was boiling like a big kettle of fish.

Hardly anyone was still sitting in their seat, and the men in particular were shouting and bawling so loudly that the crier could hardly make himself heard.

The highlight of the day was coming up: the fight of a man named Nicanor against Nemesis, the gladiatrix.

Nicanor meant 'victor.' A boldly chosen name, and Nicanor lived up to it. He was a free gladiator who was not bound to any school, but could only be enticed into a performance in return for extremely generous fees.

He performed as a *thraex*, a somewhat lighter fighter than the murmillo, with a helmet and a small rectangular shield. In addition, he wore high greaves and was armed with a curved sword that allowed him to thrust behind the shield of his opponent. His upper body was naked, his hips covered by a loincloth. Sweat was already shining on his muscular arms when he entered the arena.

Nicanor had defeated about three quarters of his opponents in past fights, and every spectator in the arena knew about his achievements. The battle statistics of all participating gladiators had already been announced in advance of the games on large boards and murals in front of the amphitheater, in the forum, in the market, and by various criers.

So Nicanor was definitely in favor with the audience, but it was his opponent today that all eyes focused on when he entered the arena. Or rather, when *she* entered the arena, because his opponent was none other than Nemesis, the gladiatrix.

In terms of her equipment, she certainly looked similar to a thraex. Her legendary Amazonian sword also had a strong curve, but she wore only light bandages on her legs and did not fight bare-chested. I had already witnessed fights in which female gladiators had competed against each other with their breasts exposed, but Nemesis preferred to cover her feminine charms. It seemed to me that she wanted to wow the audience—like her male competitors—with her fighting skills instead of her bare skin.

I must admit that I admired this woman for her daredevilry. Not only had she—also a free gladiator—signed up for a duel against a hero like Nicanor, but she was also fighting in these games for the second time today, having faced Mevia yesterday. Such an engagement was quite unusual, even for men.

Everyone was eagerly waiting to see how she would hold up against Nicanor after making relatively short work of Mevia yesterday. But Mevia was a novice, while Nicanor had to be considered a master of his trade.

She was dramatically inferior to the thraex in height and weight. Like Hilarius before her in his fight against Telephus, she could only rely on agility and endurance to stand a chance against Nicanor. In terms of muscular strength she was no match for him, even though she was quite sturdily built for a woman.

The fight that broke out between the two as soon as the

referee opened the arena was one of the best I have ever seen in any amphitheater. The spectators forgot their resentment and cheered the two on as if their own lives or deaths had been at stake.

Both Nicanor and the gladiatrix immediately went all out, daring bold advances, parrying masterfully, and pulling off feints that made the people cry out in amazement.

But then—out of the blue—Nicanor suddenly collapsed.

He had just retreated after a failed advance against Nemesis, so was standing a good ten feet away from her when it happened. He suddenly swayed, brought his sword arm against his forehead, and seemed to want to tear his helmet from his head. Nemesis, seizing the opportunity, charged at him.

But before she could reach him, Nicanor went down on his knees, fell forward—and remained motionless on the sand at the gladiatrix's feet.

The referee rushed to him, the masses screaming at the tops of their lungs.

"The witch has struck him down with a dark spell! Kill her!" a booming male voice could be heard from one of the upper tiers—which was immediately joined by many others, just as loudly.

"Jupiter is on her side!" a brave woman further in front tried to side with the gladiatrix. "He hurled one of his lightning bolts down on Nicanor!" She, too, was cheered.

"Get up, Nicanor, you weakling," others roared.

In front of me, Marcellus, Cornix and Iulianus rose from their seats and tried to calm the people with words. But their attempts at appeasement had no chance against the wild clamor. The amphitheater had turned into a seething witches' cauldron.

Chaos broke out in the stands. Men and women were on their feet, shouting as if possessed and gesticulating so violently that some of the noses or ribs of their seat neighbors were surely being broken.

"Finish the woman, Nicanor! Stand up and fight like a man!"

"She truly is Nemesis, the goddess of vengeance!"

"Why don't you take your clothes off already and let us see your boobs, sweetie!"

"Come play with my sword, you hot cat!"

"To the stake with her, to the cross!"

"She is a disgrace to all women!"

And so on.

The referee, after only a brief examination of the fallen thraex, turned to the tribune and gave Marcellus a clear sign. No one had to decide Nicanor's fate; he was dead.

VII

I had to use all my powers of persuasion on Marcellus before he finally allowed Layla to accompany me to the ludus in the evening. Gladiator schools were an inglorious place, where a Roman nobleman would not normally direct his steps. But Marcellus had never cared much for such class barriers. How else could he have loved Layla, a former slave?

He didn't miss the opportunity to accompany us, either—probably because he was as eager as I to shed light on the strange events of the day.

First a gladiator—Mevia, who had died in the night following a fight, having suffered only minor injuries. Shortly after, a sudden mass death among the condemned, although they had been well guarded in the ludus. And then there was the completely incomprehensible death of Nicanor this afternoon. In the middle of the fight, without the gladiatrix even touching him with her sword.

Thinking about it more carefully, the fight between Telephus and Hilarius had also been strange. Telephus, a veteran and celebrated hero of the arena, had fought like a coward: lame and overcautious.

Was there an evil poison at work in all these cases? Or even a spell?

While Marcellus, Layla and I walked the perhaps hundred steps from the amphitheater to the gladiator school,

I turned to my friend with a question. Behind it was only idle curiosity, but once a snoop, always a snoop, I suppose.

"Tell me, Marcellus, what Iulianus and Cornix whispered to you earlier—when it came to the fate of Hilarius. How would they have decided? Death or pardon?"

A smile flitted across my friend's features. He looked first at me, then at Layla.

"You two really are born detectores," he said. "Always asking questions and snooping around. Even though I'm still getting used to your new job title."

His gaze lingered on Layla's beautiful dark features. "Which is not to say that I find this kind of activity suitable for a woman," he added quickly.

It felt like the hundredth time that he'd expressed himself in this vein.

Layla acknowledged his remark with an apologetic smile. She was not a quarrelsome or stubborn woman. That is to say, she *was* stubborn, alright, but she always used to assert her wishes and ideas in a meek and sometimes very inconspicuous way. Sometimes, in the end, you even had the impression that you'd wanted it that way yourself all along.

I don't know how she did it; both Marcellus and I were pure putty in her hands.

Finally, the legate answered my question: "Cornix spoke in favor of pardoning Hilarius. He indicated to me that we'd owe Varro fifty times the fee agreed upon for the fighter if we wanted to see him die."

"A very practical argument," I said with a nod.

"Of course. I am certainly not the enemy of my purse," Marcellus replied. "But neither do I condone sacrificing a brave fighter merely because the public is in a bad mood. That, by the way, would have been the advice of Iulianus, the words he whispered to me. *Give the people the blood they want to see, as compensation for the disappointing executions at noon.*"

"So he wanted Hilarius dead," Layla cut in. "Hmm, interesting." Her eyes twinkled in a strange way.

I didn't know what was going on inside her mind—as it often happened to me with women in general and Layla in particular—but I didn't give it a second thought, either.

We had reached the ludus. At the pillared entrance gate, a guard let us in with a polite greeting.

Varro had already given us a tour of his school once, when Marcellus and his co-sponsors had decided to host the current games. The facility was therefore already familiar to me.

The ludus resembled a square, well-fortified homestead with a large courtyard and an adjacent campus, also surrounded by a wall. On this large open space were grouped some smaller farm buildings, the stables, as well as an area that now housed the cages with the beasts for the arena. On the respective days of their fight, they were transported to special dungeons in the underground section of the amphitheater, but there was no room for every animal there.

The east wing of the building, which one entered through the main gate, housed the administrative and reception rooms of the ludus, as well as a large training hall for the gladiators that could be heated in winter.

Varro himself did not live in the school; he had a neat little country villa built a little further west, where he lived in abundant luxury for a lanista. His wife must truly have left him a handsome fortune.

Well, probably his dear deceased had not wanted to miss any living comfort herself during her lifetime, when the villa had been built. Especially after having to move with her husband to Vindobona, the very end of the world.

The southern part of the ludus contained the prison wing. Here tiny cells were lined up, housing the enslaved gladiators, as well as those unfortunates who were awaiting execution in the arena.

On the west side, there was a dining and recreation room where all the residents of the ludus could gather: the gladiators and trainers of the school, those to be executed when games were held, and the house slaves and guards. People ate and lived together here when they were not working on their martial arts in the training hall or in the large courtyard of the ludus.

And training was done here in the school almost all the time, for many hours a day. The *doctores*—that was the name of the trainers of the gladiators, not to be confused with the medicus—were ruthless men and always tried to get the best out of their charges.

There was even a separate wooden training arena in the courtyard, where certain spectators—for example, interested sponsors—could inspect the quality of the local gladiators.

In addition, the west wing housed the quarters of the guards and house slaves, as well as some more spacious and better equipped gladiatorial quarters that extended into the north wing.

These chambers were occupied by the free gladiators

and those guests like Nemesis who arrived for the games only for a few days or weeks.

Finally, in the north wing of the school, there was a small but well-equipped hospital run by the medicus, and the school's bathhouse, as well as a few rooms for scribes and other administrative staff.

Varro, the lanista, was immediately on hand that evening to give us a proper welcome and to have his slaves bring us some refreshments. The evening air was as mild as on a summer's day.

After we'd exchanged a few pleasantries with the lanista, and he'd assured us at least ten times that everything would run perfectly tomorrow, Optimus appeared as if on cue.

I asked him to lead us to Atticus, the school's medic. We would most likely be able to learn more about the suspicious deaths from him.

Varro did not raise any objections; he seemed relieved that we were not angry with him for the less-than-perfect second day of the games, and even wanted to help investigate the unfortunate events at his school.

Every professional ludus employed an excellent medicus. The training and upkeep of gladiators was a costly affair, so a wise lanista invested in the best medical care for his fighters.

Minor injuries sustained by a gladiator in the arena were carefully washed with vinegar, larger ones were skillfully stitched up, and if a wound bled too profusely, they even resorted to red-hot irons to close it again.

In addition to the medicus, most gladiatorial schools had their own masseur and in-house baths, to keep the fighters in the best possible condition.

However there was no question of the gladiators being in good shape at Varro's ludus at the moment: two fighters, including a very expensive one, were dead, and apparently for no reason—Mevia and Nicanor.

Optimus told us that the slaves and servants of Varro were already talking about dark magic, of a curse that lay on the school.

Nicanor was not even a fighter belonging to this ludus, but a free gladiator whom Varro had hired only for the glory of these special games. In this case, the lanista had not suffered any financial loss, since he had not invested years in the training and maintenance of the man.

In fact, quite the opposite; Nicanor had died during a battle, so Marcellus and his two co-sponsors owed Varro the painfully expensive fee that was due for a fallen gladiator.

As for all the talk of dark magic and a curse from the gods, I'd expected nothing less. The common people were always particularly quick to hand with this fear. But perhaps I should admit at this point that I had also been inclined toward such an explanation at one or another time in earlier murder cases. At least at the beginning. In the end Layla and I had always been able to find an earthly explanation for the various deaths.

But from the beginning, this time, I did not believe that the immortals could be to blame. Behind these strange deaths that cast their shadow over the games and the ludus, there had to be an insidious poison. At least that was my assumption.

This conjecture was to be immediately confirmed by

Atticus, the school's medic, to whom Optimus duly led us.

Atticus was a fairly young fellow, a native of Byzantium in the eastern part of the empire, with bronze skin, bushy brows, and strong but nimble hands. His Latin was marked by a rolling, somewhat comical accent, but he looked like someone who knew his subject.

Layla once again could not hold on to herself. She was already asking the medicus her first question, even before he had properly greeted us. "Apart from Nicanor and Mevia, have any other gladiators in the school fallen ill or even died?"

The Medicus first looked surprised that a woman had spoken up, before Marcellus the commander of the legion could do so, and that he did not rein her in.

But Atticus quickly composed himself. If I wasn't mistaken, an amused grin flitted across his features for a brief moment, but when he answered, his words sounded serious.

"You heard about the convicts who perished? Seven of them died this morning—just before some of the men were to be led into the arena, to lay down their lives there."

He fell silent for a moment, then raised his head and looked at Marcellus. Naturally, he considered him to be the interlocutor to whom he had to politely address himself, due to his high rank as legate.

"I haven't had a chance to take a closer look at the bodies of those men. I had to tend to some wounds, and I subjected Mevia's remains to a closer inspection. Also, I examined the dead Nicanor, who was just transferred to me from the amphitheater earlier."

He narrowed his eyes, making them look even darker. "I

could swear that poison was involved in the deaths of *both* gladiators."

VIII

I was not surprised when Layla rejoined the conversation at this point. She engaged the medicus in a long technical discussion about poisons, their preparation, administration, symptoms, and the time lag of their effectiveness.

It turned out that Atticus was quite familiar with the subject, but Layla's knowledge clearly exceeded his. An expression of astonishment formed on his face, which became more pronounced with every word my former lover spoke.

Perhaps I should mention at this point that Layla was a fanatical reader, who had spent entire days and even weeks in my library over the past few months educating herself in preparation for our newfound vocation as murder investigators. And that I'd kept several of my servants busy, tracking down and bringing in the appropriate books for her.

Of course, Marcellus also had a small, high-quality collection of books in his legate's palace. But he probably would not have thought of getting his beloved the reading material she thirsted for: descriptions of crimes, technical works on Roman law, and especially books on poisons.

When Layla came to visit me, she often spoke to me of poisonings. I heard about lore that went back centuries, about murder cases that some meticulous chronicler—often even a well-known philosopher—had recorded in minute detail, about executions in other parts of the province or even in Rome, when someone had been convicted of murder with a deadly substance, and so on. Layla kept emphasizing how old and widespread the art of mixing poisons was.

I learned—from the mouth of a woman who looked so delicate and innocent!—for example, about the poisoned arrows of the Scythians, who had already struck down their enemies in this way half a millennium ago. They did not use any vegetable or animal substances, no; they coated their arrows with the poison that formed in corpses.

I shuddered at the thought, but Layla found it most delightful. She also spoke of Persians and Greeks poisoning wells, and the other watering places of their enemies, with animal carcasses, and that the famous Hannibal once had vessels with poisonous snakes hurled at enemy ships in a naval battle.

I learned even more about famous poisoners. Most of them were women, which gave me pause—and Layla concluded: "We probably don't even know the *real* geniuses among poisoners, which is a shame. Because their deeds will probably go undetected forever."

What a thought. I couldn't come up with an appropriate answer.

"The perfect crime," she mused, looking like a cat feasting on particularly creamy milk.

As if that were not enough, Layla had also asked me to plant a small garden near my house. There, as soon as the winter was over, she began to experiment with the cultivation of poisonous plants. She instructed my slaves to catch her a few dozen rats and mice in the stables, and on these unfortunate creatures she tested the first powders, elixirs and tinctures that she had mixed herself. It was the best way to educate herself in the field of poisons, she explained to me.

It was understandable that she wanted to plant the garden on my estate, wasn't it? When I imagined such a poisonous garden blossoming and flourishing in the middle of the legionary camp of Vindobona, directly behind the legate's palace, I had to smile. Poor Marcellus, what would his legionaries have thought of him?

Even without the soldiers learning of Layla's darkest interests, there was always talk of the 'black sphinx' whom the legate kept as his mistress. I think that most of the legionaries—fellows who are almost as superstitious as house slaves—saw her as a dangerous witch who had cast a spell over their commander. And that notion could not be completely dismissed.

Layla did not want to shock or compromise her lover, so I was her accomplice when it came to her poison mixing and other unsavory experiments.

In any case, the rodents on which Layla was so joyfully testing her powders and tinctures were already beginning to avoid my property. It had probably gotten around on their secret grapevine that one lived most dangerously here.

But I want to report further regarding the conversation we had with Atticus, the medic of the gladiator school. He had already formed a theory on how and why the deaths had occurred, and who had to be responsible.

"I think the goal was to weaken the two gladiators for the

fight," he explained to us after the discussion on poisons with Layla was finally over. "I don't think it really worked on Mevia. He didn't get sick until much later, and then he died during the night, which probably wasn't what the poisoner had had in mind. It only attracted unnecessary attention. So the next morning, the perpetrator decided to better adjust his dose—and experimented on the condemned. At least it was humane that he used them, and did not poison the inhabitants of the ludus indiscriminately."

"Except that after his experiments, as you call them, he left half a dozen corpses," I objected. "Unnecessary attention, my ass! I guess it went badly wrong, then."

Atticus tilted his head. "I suppose it did, but that's what can happen during experiments. And our perpetrator may not be aware of how differently people can react to the same poison, the same dose. One may die in agony, the next may merely become seriously ill, and a third may escape completely unscathed. But nevertheless, our murderess educated herself further. After all, she poisoned Nicanor just enough that he collapsed in the arena. It was only her bad luck that she did not attack him right before he died, as I've been told. But otherwise, this murder was probably much more skillfully executed than that of Mevia's."

"Did you say *murderess*?" asked Layla. "So you think Nemesis is behind these acts?"

"Who else?" Atticus promptly replied. "She had to compete in the arena against those two men, didn't she? And she wants to prove to all the world what an outstanding Amazon she is. Someone who can take on even seasoned fighters."

"So are you saying she's a fraudster?" interjected Marcellus. "She weakens her enemies with poison so that she can more easily finish them off in the arena?"

The medicus nodded. "She can move freely here at the ludus. Quite inconspicuously these days, since she's staying here. She has had access to the food and drink of both the gladiators and the condemned. Even though the food for the two groups is different, of course—the fighters get nutritious grain porridge, plus their potion is fortified with bone ash to strengthen their constitution. Personally, I have devised a new recipe that..."

He interrupted himself, lowering his head modestly. "It doesn't matter," he murmured.

"Well anyway," he continued right after, "I managed to secure some leftover food from the breakfast of the condemned convicts. For those who were to be brought to the arena at noon today, it should have been their last pleasure before death—not their premature end. I will find out if this food has been laced with poison, first thing in the morning. For tonight, you will have to excuse me; I have some fighters to attend to."

IX

"I think we should have a word with this Amazon," I suggested once we were back amongst ourselves.

Only Optimus was still standing by our side, and he strongly disagreed with the medicus's conclusions.

"Nemesis certainly wouldn't do anything like that," he grumbled. "She has no need to poison her opponents."

Layla gave him an interested look, but then we all directed our steps toward the west wing of the school, where—as I have already described—the somewhat more spacious chambers of the free gladiators were located.

Nemesis inhabited such a chamber, bordering the western exit of the school. Through the narrow gate located here, one first entered the campus near to the animal cages and the stables, and finally came to a smaller gate to the outside, which was usually kept locked.

After all, one did not want to risk an enslaved fighter, or even one of the condemned, coming up with the stupid idea of seeking his salvation in flight.

Seen up close, Nemesis was on the one hand a woman of ravishing beauty, but on the other she had something devious, cold and dangerous about her. Her hair and eyes were a dark brown, her lips full and beautifully curved.

The most extraordinary thing about her, however, was a fiery red mark on the left side of her neck. It stretched a good hand's breadth from top to bottom, almost as if a bolt of lightning from Jupiter, the father of the gods, had seared her skin, giving her the superhuman strength with which she defied men in the arena.

Nemesis received us with suspicion and a pinched mouth as Optimus led us into her room.

Marcellus, as usual, didn't beat around the bush or even dwell on pleasantries.

"Step aside, we want to search your chamber," he commanded the gladiatrix as soon as she'd opened her door for us.

For a moment, a rebellious spark glowed in the Amazon's dark eyes. She straightened her back and I thought that she would stand in the way of my friend or even attack him.

But then she thought better of it. She might be hotheaded, but she was no fool. If a legate of the legions appeared in your chamber, you were already in plenty of trouble. Attacking him could get you put into the arena—this time without weapons—faster than you could utter your own name.

With a nod of his head, Marcellus commanded Optimus to take a closer look at the chamber's sparse furnishings.

The floor of the room was decorated with a pretty, if not very artistic, mosaic. In addition, there was a chest that the gladiatrix probably used in her travels, and a bedstead made of wood and iron. In one corner of the room there was a simple table and a matching stool.

Optimus hesitated for a moment. Was I mistaken, or did he actually give the gladiatrix an apologetic look before preparing to open her chest?

"May I ask what you seek from me?" Nemesis addressed

Marcellus.

Her gaze grazed his face, then wandered over to me, finally coming to rest on Layla's ebony countenance.

Layla gave the fighter a furtive smile. What could our black sphinx be thinking now?

Marcellus, meanwhile, deigned to answer the gladiatrix: "We seek that means by which you weaken your opponents," he said straightforwardly. "Or the utensils for the spell you cast on them. Best you give them up willingly. Then you shall enjoy a quick death—without any torture."

He did not speak further. His gaze wandered aimlessly around the room for a moment. Was he, one who loved to watch elaborate executions in the arena, already thinking about what very special end he wanted to give the gladiatrix?

Nemesis's eyes widened, but she did not reply. One could not hope for a quick confession of guilt from this woman, no matter what she might have done, or how much Marcellus tried to threaten her. Her will seemed to be as strong as her legendary sword.

Optimus rummaged through the gladiatrix's chest, but then indicated to the legate with a shake of his head that there was nothing suspicious inside. He next turned to the bed, looked under the mattress, lifted the blanket....

Nemesis pinched her lips together. The accusation Marcellus had made was clearly an insult to her honor.

"You think I have to cheat to achieve my victories?" she hurled at him. "Ha! Just because I'm a woman?"

She straightened up to her full height—which, however, reached no further than under the eyes of us men. She looked first at me, then at Marcellus.

"Proud barbarian, noble legate, you think I can't defeat a man? I'll take you both on!" she literally spat in our faces. "And at the same time!"

Before any of us could reply, she added, "Do you want to give the crowds in the arena a true spectacle? Then how about a fight tomorrow? You two against me. Do you dare?"

For a moment it was dead silent in the room. The gladiatrix stood there with her chin thrust forward, while—I have to admit—I was speechless. And probably my friend, too. Only Layla continued to smile, now even more furtively. This Amazon was really foolhardy. Not to say tired of life.

Marcellus was immediately in control again. "Watch your tongue, gladiatrix," he replied to the fighter with cold anger in his eyes. "Neither of us will dishonor ourselves and step into the sands of the arena! And you should be careful that you don't find yourself in the amphitheater tomorrow without your weapons, face to face with some hungry beasts. Then you can prove how good you really are!"

X

Optimus completed his search, nodding courteously to Marcellus, but shaking his head again after he had finished.

"I could not find anything, legate, that would connect her in any way to the crimes," he announced in a very neutral tone.

"What crimes are you talking about?" interjected Nemesis before Marcellus could answer.

She moderated her tone a bit and then added, "Maybe someone can tell me what I'm actually being accused of? You can't really believe that I hex my opponents, right?" She looked at me, presumably in order not to enrage Marcellus any further.

She knew that as a gladiator she was very far down the Roman pecking order; not to say at the very bottom. Only prostitutes and criminals enjoyed a lower standing than gladiators—even if the fighters were celebrated like heroes in the arena. In everyday life, they were considered the outcasts of society. What the Roman philosophers thought of women who dishonored their sex and virtue by fighting in the arena, I prefer not to quote here.

Layla took it upon herself to put the gladiatrix in the picture regarding what Atticus thought about the death of her two opponents. She also mentioned that we held the same opinion.

"*Poisoned?*" Nemesis repeated incredulously.

Layla nodded and then described to her the deaths of the seven convicts, who had presumably fallen victim to the same murderer as Mevia and Nicanor.

"And you think *I* killed those men?" Nemesis roared with renewed anger. "In such a cowardly manner, and from ambush? And those convicts as well, poor sods who had long since forfeited their lives? Who only faced death at the stake or in the claws of a bear? Why, by all the gods, should I wish to kill them?"

"To determine the correct dose of your poison so that Nicanor would die at the right time today?" I retorted. "Not like Mevia yesterday, who succumbed to the insidious substance only in the night, long after the fight."

Nemesis snorted, but said nothing. She seemed lost in thought, which prompted me to ask another question: "Didn't you notice that Mevia and Nicanor were weakened, shall we say? That they weren't fighting you with their full fervor?"

The gladiatrix brushed a dark strand of hair from her forehead.

"I fought both of them for the first time," she replied after a brief silence. "I can't judge what else they might have been capable of. But I will grant you that Nicanor today—how shall I put it?—that he seemed a little awkward, for such an experienced fighter as he was supposed to be. Of course I asked around in advance, about his fighting style, his strengths, his weaknesses. Such knowledge can make the difference between life and death, in the sands of the arena. Every self-respecting gladiator prepares in this way, I assure you."

"I can understand that," I said.

"I have seen most gladiators fight with my own eyes," she continued, now in a somewhat calmer tone. "But with Nicanor, I had not yet had the opportunity. Therefore I had to rely on hearsay."

"I'm just wasting my time here," Marcellus interrupted her bad-temperedly. "You may be a murderess, gladiatrix, but you're certainly not stupid. And you can move freely in the ludus, and even throughout the city. If you wanted to mix poison, you could easily find an undisturbed place to do the deed. And you also had enough time to get rid of any remains of it after the murders. Therefore it doesn't prove anything that we've found nothing in your chamber."

He directed the next words to Layla and me. "If you want, I'll have Varro turn the whole ludus upside down, but now I have a dinner date. Cornix has invited Iulianus and me, and of course I accepted."

"I would like to look around a bit more," I replied, but then I was not on the guest list at the supper anyway. I was a somewhat respectable neighbor for the inhabitants of Vindobona, but I did not belong to the illustrious circles which Marcellus, Cornix or Iulianus used to frequent.

It didn't sadden me in this case, because the mystery of the poisonings at the ludus appealed to me far more than a culinary climax and the obligatory drinking binge that inevitably tended to follow such occasions.

Musicians, dancers, acrobats, a boring recitation of some intellectual effusions from the master of the house's pen.... In the villas of Vindobona's richest they knew how to entertain themselves, and not much worse than in Rome.

But I could easily afford similar pleasures myself, if I'd felt like it, and in more pleasant company.

The fact that Marcellus, Cornix, and Iulianus were co-sponsoring the games seemed to have deepened the acquaintance of the three men. Or were they even friends, now?

I liked the suave Cornix, even if I envied his outstanding success as a merchant. Iulianus, on the other hand, the arrogant new rich, was not after my taste.

But as a legate, I guess you had to think differently. Or should I say, more diplomatically?

Marcellus had mastered this art splendidly. He seemed to get along well with everyone who had rank and name in Vindobona. But he was self-confident enough to cultivate even unusual relationships that were personally close to his heart. With Layla, for example, or with me. And that's what I appreciated about him.

Layla joined me, asking Marcellus to let her look around the ludus with me a little longer. I promised the legate I'd accompany her back to his palace later. He finally approved with a generous nod of his head.

I'm sure he didn't like the fact that his beloved was snooping around in a ludus, of all places, but on the other hand I suspected that he too wanted the mystery of the poisonings to be solved. He had no official need to take action as legate—after all, only a few criminals and two gladiators had been killed, not respected citizens of the town—but he too was tormented by curiosity about what this strange case was all about. That's how well I knew my friend.

When Marcellus stormed out of the chamber of the

gladiatrix with toga flowing behind him, we also wanted to turn to leave. But as we did so, we spotted one of the guard slaves outside in the corridor, who seemed to have been waiting for us. He was a roundish guy with an almost bald skull and an overly fleshy nose.

His gaze flitted first to Optimus, to whom he was subordinate in the ludus, then over to me. He clearly had something on his mind, and seemed overzealous. Or was he just interested in a generous tip?

"Pardon me, sir," he addressed me, "I heard from Atticus, our medicus, that the witch poisoned Nicanor. And some other men," he added.

Nemesis, who had overheard the insult, took a step out of her chamber.

I was just quick enough to intervene, otherwise she would probably have made short work of the guy, and with nothing but her bare fists.

Optimus came to the rescue. He put one of his muscular hands on the gladiatrix's arm to stop her.

She backed off, brushing his hand away as if an annoying insect had settled on her skin. But her gesture was gentle, not violent.

"I want to hear what the man has to say," I said, then challenged the guard to tell us what was on his mind.

The fellow turned to Optimus with a rather uncertain look. "You can confirm it, can't you? That the, um, gladiatrix had a quarrel last night with Nicanor. If you hadn't intervened, she would have killed him for sure," he blurted out. His watery blue eyes widened.

I had a suspicion that the man was rather fond of undiluted wine, but if Optimus could confirm his words, I would naturally be willing to believe him.

The reaction of my good Optimus, however, was somehow strange. He didn't seem the least bit pleased that the guard had addressed us.

However, now was not the time to find out why. I gave the fleshy-nosed man my attention and asked him to continue talking.

A fight between Nicanor and the gladiatrix, and at night, far from the arena? That was interesting. Possibly a motive for at least one of the poisonings could be found here.

"What was the argument about?" I asked the guard slave.

But he knew no answer to that. He only repeated what he had already said: that Nicanor and Nemesis had gotten into a fight, and that Optimus had intervened heroically.

XI

"Maybe you can tell us what turned you and Nicanor against each other?" Layla addressed the gladiatrix directly, who was still lurking in the background like a lioness ready to pounce—and probably hadn't forgotten that the guard had called her a witch.

Nemesis eyed Layla with undisguised curiosity. It could not have escaped her notice that she was looking at a woman who was just as unusual as herself. Perhaps for this reason she gave the information quite willingly.

"Nicanor wanted to make sure that I was not a hermaphrodite. With these words he entered my chamber—and threw himself upon me. He mocked me, saying that a real woman could never have so much strength and skill as I had proven to have in the arena time and again."

She raised her head and laughed harshly. "Apparently he'd studied my fights, made inquiries about them, and asked spectators and former opponents of mine. I guess he was afraid I could be a dangerous challenge for him after all!"

Her dark eyes narrowed. "Then, when he realized I was a woman after all and not a hermaphrodite, he wanted love favors, if you want to put it that way."

Her tone sounded almost bored, but there was an expression of disgust on her face. "When I was not willing to grant it to him freely, he wanted to take it by force."

She gave Optimus a look that I was not able to interpret. There didn't seem to be much gratitude in it, but something like ... acknowledgment, for coming to her aid against Nicanor's assault, as she'd just described. Even if Nemesis certainly believed that she didn't need any man's help.

"I was just about to let Nicanor taste my fists when *he* came storming into the room." She pointed her hand at Optimus. "Which was lucky for Nicanor," she added dryly. "I could have killed him; I merely refrained from doing so because I didn't want any trouble with Varro."

She clicked her tongue and turned to me. "As you can imagine, I'm used to such favors. As a gladiatrix, I'm fair game for any man, rich or poor, old or young, slave or senator. In the past, when I was still tied to a school, I had to deal with that, but now as a free woman, no more. If a man wants to lay a hand on me, it's over my dead body!"

This explanation did not come as a surprise to me; Nemesis's passionate words may have been true, or at least they were a plausible excuse. Female fighters—even those far less attractive than Nemesis—were all too often the victims of rape in the gladiatorial schools of the empire. Be it by the guards, by other gladiators, the lanista himself ... or even his sponsors. At the traditional banquet on the eve of the games, to which the fighters were also invited, sponsors almost notoriously used to assault a gladiatrix, if one were present.

I had wondered at the opening feast of our games, which had taken place a few days ago in the house of Iulianus, that Nemesis wasn't present. Now, however, it occurred to me that Varro, the lanista, had probably made a wise decision in this regard. His sponsors might have been disappointed that they couldn't get their hands on such an exotic Amazon—but this certainly had caused Varro less inconvenience than if Nemesis had stood up to a rapist. She was probably not only capable of resisting, but also very determined to do so. Better a disgruntled sponsor than a dead one, Varro had probably thought to himself.

Of course, I would not have thought Marcellus capable of such an atrocity, but Cornix and Iulianus would certainly have been much less reluctant to 'have a good time' with a gladiatrix, as they might have put it.

"Can you confirm what Nemesis claims?" I asked Optimus. "That Nicanor was going to have his way with her, and she was merely fighting back?"

"Yes, sir," he answered me in a very formal tone. Something was definitely wrong with him.

I turned back to Nemesis. "So that means you had another reason for wanting Nicanor dead, and not just because he was your opponent in the arena. Maybe you wanted to poison him in revenge for his night-time assault?"

"I wanted to get back at him for believing any woman was fair game for his lusts," Nemesis admitted bluntly. "That's why I swore he wouldn't leave the arena alive today. But I didn't have to use poison to kill him," she added emphatically. "I would have finished him off with my sword, I swear to you! It may be that the gods punished him and struck him down in front of everyone before I could, though."

She glared at me challengingly. Then she added, "Are you done with me now? I've had a long day ... and I want to start my journey home in the morning."

She was already turning on the threshold, but I was not so easily dismissed.

"You will not be traveling anywhere tomorrow," I said. "You will stay here at the ludus until we solve these poisonings. If you are innocent, you may go your way after that. If not...."

I left my words unfinished. She knew what I meant, what fate awaited her if we convicted her of being a murderer.

She shot me another challenging look. "You have no authority over me, barbarian!" she hissed.

"Would you rather have the legate's soldiers take you prisoner? And bring you to trial for murder?" I retorted.

"But you don't have a thing on me!"

I didn't reply; I didn't intend to get involved in a verbal duel with this Amazon. Instead, I just gave her a look—but she knew how to interpret it.

Suspects have already been sentenced to death on the cross or ad bestias on the basis of far less conclusive evidence than is available against you. I let her know that without having to move my lips. She was not a naive young girl; she had lived in the Roman world long enough to understand me, and to know that I was right.

So she finally complied, albeit snorting. "Then I'll just stay," she announced, disappearing into her room and slamming the door behind her.

I left this rudeness unatoned, exchanged another wordless glance with Layla, then left the west wing with her.

Optimus, who was following behind us, probably thought that we would now leave the ludus. It was getting late, and he offered to give us a guard from the school on the way home. Layla and I were both traveling without an entourage.

But I was not ready to turn my back on the gladiator school just yet. I asked Optimus to unlock the gate that led out onto the campus.

There, under the starry sky, in the immediate vicinity of the animal cages that held the magnificent beasts for the arena, I addressed my friend—whose sincerity and reliability I actually appreciated very much. Here, apart from a few lions or wolves, no one would overhear our conversation.

"Listen, Optimus," I began without mincing my words, "when were you going to tell us about this incident between Nicanor and the gladiatrix? I can't help thinking that you were going to keep it quiet, if the guy with the fleshy nose hadn't mentioned it."

Optimus contorted his face as if I had trampled him underfoot.

"I was going to tell you, sir!" he exclaimed. "I would not have concealed it."

He hesitated, biting his lips. "But this incident, this altercation ... that doesn't mean Nemesis poisoned the guy! You realize that, I hope?" He gave me a questioning—no, an almost pleading look.

Then he continued unasked, "She really is as outstanding a fighter as everyone says, Thanar. She doesn't need to resort to poisons to defeat her opponents. You can take my word for that!"

"Oh, and how would you know?"

An expression of embarrassment spread across the features of the good Optimus.

"I am not a gladiator," he began hesitantly, "but I was once a good fighter, too, when I was still serving in the legion. And so a few days ago I challenged the gladiatrix to a practice fight, here at the ludus, shortly after she'd joined us."

I couldn't believe my ears. "You did *what*?"

It took me a moment to process his words. Then I continued, "I must say, your enthusiasm for the games really goes a long way, my dear friend."

He grimaced sheepishly. "Well, um, of course I don't do that with every guest gladiator who visits our school. Only with Nemesis—it was the first time. But I just wanted to know how well she really fights."

"And?" I asked, by now a little amused.

His embarrassment grew. "I hate to say it, Thanar, but she defeated me in no time. I was very glad that we only were fighting with wooden weapons."

A smile flitted across his face. "Do you understand, sir? This woman has no need to poison anyone. I give you my word on that."

"You're quite impressed by Nemesis," Layla intervened abruptly. "Aren't you, dear Optimus? And I don't mean merely as a fighter."

I swear by all the gods that Optimus turned dark red at this point, like a schoolboy who had been caught stealing apples!

I looked at Layla in surprise, and she gave me that smile for which I used to call her 'my black sphinx.' Inscrutable, knowing ... and still very confusing for me, I must confess.

Optimus said: "This Nicanor fellow had already been skulking around the corridor near her chamber for several nights, starting as soon as Nemesis arrived here at the ludus. I knew he was up to something, which is why I kept an eye on the gladiatrix's room."

"One might wonder, however, why you were out in that corridor at night in the first place, and discovered Nicanor there," Layla objected in a meek, if mischievous, tone. "After all, the free gladiators don't need to be guarded, right?"

Now Optimus really started to stutter. "I ... just wanted to make sure no one messed with Nemesis. You know how it is; you heard it from her own mouth. When you're a gladiatrix, you're fair game."

"Didn't you just tell me what an outstanding fighter she is?" I objected. "How could she need your protection when she could defeat you so easily? Admit it, dear friend, you have your eye on this beautiful Amazon!"

Layla started to grin, which infected me, and eventually caught Optimus as well. Finally, all three of us were laughing, and I slapped my friend on the shoulder.

"What a woman!" he groaned. "Isn't she a regular whirlwind? An Amazon queen! A gift from the gods! Oh, I wish I could conquer her for myself."

"I'm sure it won't be easy," I replied good-humoredly— but I didn't forget that Optimus might have fallen in love with a murderess.

XII

When we finally left the ludus, two slaves of Marcellus were waiting for Layla with a wagon. Even though the legionary camp—and thus the legate's palace—was barely a quarter of a mile from the school, Layla's lover probably wanted to make certain that no harm came to her on the way home.

I didn't miss the opportunity to accompany Layla the short distance, even so, and climbed into the wagon with her. While we were rumbling through the streets of the camp suburb, which were still quite busy even at this late hour, I came to talk about something that was bothering me.

"The strange behavior of Telephus in his battle against Hilarius ... I can't get it out of my head," I told my former lover as we passed taverns and snack bars, dilapidated wooden barracks and magnificent stone townhouses. "The way he was hiding behind his shield, playing for time—it just doesn't fit the celebrated veteran he's supposed to be."

"*Supposed* to be?" asked Layla.

"Well, I saw him fight for the first time today, so I only know about his great successes from hearsay. But they speak for themselves, don't they?"

I would call myself a fan—and to some extent a connoisseur—of the games, but I was not one of those fanatical followers who traveled half the empire just so as not to miss a single battle of their favorite gladiators.

"I can't imagine that Telephus could have won so many victories—around fifty in seventy fights, wasn't it?— merely by playing for time and by tiring his opponent, as he did today. Thus he insulted the audience, who wanted to see a spectacular, daredevil fight. No, that's impossible. The audience would not pardon such a fighter if he lost to his opponent just once."

After all every gladiator, no matter how skilled, lost a fight every now and then. However, he usually did not pay for it with his life, because his supporters loudly ensured that the sponsor of those particular games pardoned him.

"So you think that Telephus was poisoned, too?" Layla asked. "Just like Mevia and Nicanor, albeit with a smaller dose? Do you believe that's why he fought in so cowardly a fashion, because he was weakened by some insidious substance?"

"Do you have a better explanation?" I replied.

She shook her head.

But then she said, "That would speak against Nemesis as the perpetrator. For why should she have poisoned Telephus? She did not fight against him, after all."

"What if she performed some sort of experiment on him, too? Like on the convicts?" I suggested.

Our wagon came to an abrupt halt because a fully loaded mule cart had cut across our right of way. Our draft horse, a well-fed animal with a night-black coat, reared up in fright. Layla was thrown quite ungently against me.

I opened my arms as a matter of course to catch her— until I realized how inappropriate it was. But I had been so absorbed in our debate about Telephus that I had simply reacted out of habit.

So I let go of Layla, moved away from her a bit, and resumed our conversation. Our wagon picked up speed again, while the slave who was steering it cursed after the mule driver.

"Hmm," I pondered, casting doubt on the hypothesis I had just formed myself: "What would an experiment on Telephus have done for the gladiatrix? She herself was already down in the arena vault when he started his fight. So however he might have reacted to the poison—the result was worthless for Nemesis, because she would not know about it in time. She could not watch Telephus fight Hilarius, she was already busy preparing for her own performance. And by then she must have poisoned Nicanor, if she really is the guilty party."

Layla nodded as our ride together rapidly drew to a close. She didn't seem to have a better explanation for Telephus's disappointing fight, either. Could it be that the famous veteran had simply had a very bad day?

At the gate of the legionary camp I said goodbye to Layla, climbed out of the wagon and made my way to the bridge that led across the Danubius. My house was located on the northern bank of the river.

Of course, I could have made the trip to the amphitheater this morning on horseback or in one of my own wagons. A self-respecting Roman nobleman would never have traveled a whole mile or so on foot, but I was no such snob. I liked to occasionally get out on my own and stretch my legs a bit, especially at night and when I had a crime to ponder. So this little walk would come in handy.

While I crossed the Danubius dry-footed and still had

not found an explanation for the strange fighting behavior of Telephus, my thoughts wandered to another mystery, to Alma Philonica, the widow I'd been thinking about so often in the last few months. She attracted me as Layla had done in the past—and she was just as much a mystery to me.

How did Alma really feel about me? What were her plans for the future? When would she finally arrive in Vindobona, since she had promised to pay me another visit? According to the letter she'd sent me before her departure, she should have arrived by now, provided the journey had been without obstacles. Which, unfortunately, one could not always assume.

Surely nothing had happened to her? Should I have a horse saddled, gather some of my men around me and ride out to meet her, instead of worrying about a few murdered gladiators and convicts? Or would Alma then call me controlling, obsessive, and overly anxious if I made such a fuss about her arrival? After all, she was a wealthy widow and not prone to recklessness. She had certainly provided an adequate escort on her journey to Vindobona.

What would Alma say when she finally arrived at my house and found me involved in another murder case? She was certainly not a fearful woman, but still....

When I finally reached my house, I had a cup of spiced wine served to me by a slave who was still on his feet, and then went to bed—where I didn't find sleep for a long time.

XIII

The night was to end earlier—and more abruptly—than I could have guessed.

The sun had scarcely risen when an urgent visitor was announced to me: at my gate stood Rusticus, the guard slave from the ludus who had told me yesterday at noon about the sudden death of the convicts.

As I hurried from my bedroom to the atrium, where I planned to receive him, I already had a feeling that at this early hour I could not honestly hope for good news.

"Optimus sent me," he said breathlessly as I stood before him. Despite the coolness of the morning, his hair clung sticky with sweat to his high forehead, and he nervously stepped from one foot to the other.

He stammered with agitation when he tried to get to the main content of his message. "The b-beasts for the arena, sir!" he cried, "some of them got free in the night! We don't know how it happened. They got into the house, into the west wing. Optimus—"

"What about Optimus?" I interrupted him. "Nothing has happened to him, has it?"

"He ... was hurt, he was. But it's nothing serious, he assured me. Atticus took care of him. And so did the gladiatrix."

"Nemesis?" I asked—quite pointlessly. After all there was only one gladiatrix staying in the ludus. But my thoughts were still sluggish, tired from the restless night, not ready to deal with a new problem.

"She was wounded, too?"

Rusticus nodded without a word.

I pondered for a moment what to do. But the answer was obvious: I had to ride to the school, to see for myself on the spot what exactly had happened.

If Optimus had been able to spare one man to send as a messenger, and the doctor was already taking care of the wounded, then the gravest danger must already have been averted. But the question remained as to how the beasts had been released.

Someone must have had a hand in it, was the first thought that came to my mind.

"Hurry back to Optimus," I instructed the messenger. "Tell him that he can count on me immediately."

Rusticus looked relieved and stormed off.

I, on the other hand, had Faustinius awakened—my friend, the animal trader. He had been a guest in my house since he had delivered the beasts ordered for the games to Varro. Could it be that he had put the animals for the ludus in inadequate cages?

He vigorously denied this question after we'd both dressed and were setting off on horseback across the Danubius.

A good dozen of his animal catchers, who had set up their tent camp not far from my house and had actually hoped for a few days off, followed after us, with their horses and two barred wagons, to recapture the escaped beasts and bring them back to the ludus. That is, if the animals had managed to escape the walls of the ludus at all—perhaps they had merely been up to mischief within the school?

I should probably have elicited some more information from Rusticus regarding what exactly had happened in the school, but due to my drowsiness I had missed the opportunity. Anyway, we would find out soon enough.

Of course, recapturing escaped beasts was usually not one of the tasks of an animal trader. After the delivery of the animals, they were the property of the ludus and thus the responsibility of the guards there. If those men were unable to safely keep the beasts enclosed, it was usually the problem of the lanista alone.

But my friend Faustinius had immediately agreed to help. The idea that a few of his lions, bears or giant snakes could jeopardize the citizens of Vindobona drove him to the utmost haste.

"None of the beasts could have gotten free on their own," he assured me as we rode toward the school. "Never. They may be angry and hungry—which is intended, after all, to make them deliver a passable spectaculum in the arena. But their cages are sized so that the bars can withstand even the wildest rage."

I believed him. Faustinius was experienced in his business and he had no need to be stingy in the construction of his cages. He was an extremely wealthy man, and one who was careful about his reputation.

"Probably some foolish slave of the ludus left the cage doors open," he reflected, when the school's gate was already in sight. "I can't explain it any other way."

"I can, though," I said somberly.

He gave me a questioning look, but I had no time to

explain myself to him. We had reached the ludus, and we jumped out of our saddles and left our horses to a slave. The troop of Faustinius's animal catchers followed at a short distance behind us.

Rusticus and some other guard slaves from the villa were on hand, escorting my friend and his men directly to the campus so they could see the situation for themselves.

I, on the other hand, rushed to Atticus's small hospital.

I found it empty. That was a good sign, I told myself. Apparently no one had been so seriously injured in the beasts' breakout that Atticus would have to be fighting for his life here.

I finally spotted Optimus in the back of the campus, amidst the crowd of guards, house slaves and Faustinius's men.

Faustinius himself was busy inspecting the locks on the cages from which the beasts had escaped, while his men were already circling two of the lions still roaming free on the campus.

Varro the lanista was standing a little way apart and was pulling at his already thinning hair, which today was so heavily pomaded that it was literally sparkling in the morning sun.

Again and again he barked orders, but hardly anyone paid attention to them. Faustinius had taken command of the campus, and he had—as far as I could see—the situation well under control.

The shock must have paralyzed Varro and confused his senses. It was clearly written on his face.

You couldn't blame the poor man; his wonderful new gladiator school certainly did not seem to be blessed with the gods' divine favor.

Only when I looked more closely at Varro did I see, not two steps behind him, a mangled human figure lying on the ground. It was a man, as far as I could tell.

He was bloodied all over, and the tunic he must have been wearing in life hung in tatters from his limbs.

I ran a few steps in Varro's direction, toward the wounded man. Or rather, toward the dead man, because there was clearly no life left in him now. I recognized that immediately; his body had been torn to pieces by the beasts.

Gutted, was the word that forced itself on me at the sight of him.

Varro did not seem to have discovered him yet. He had given up barking orders in the meantime, but he was now trying to make himself personally useful in the midst of the animal catchers. In doing so he was obstructing Faustinius and his men rather than being really helpful.

He may have been an excellent gladiator in his day, but he would have been no good as a venator, taking on wild beasts in the arena. The animals seemed to frighten him more than any broad-shouldered giant wielding a battle axe ever had.

My gaze returned to the mangled corpse. So there had been casualties after all, even though the hospital was empty. No medicus in the world would have been able to help this poor fellow anymore.

I crouched down close to the corpse and took a closer look. Fortunately Layla was not with me this morning. I still refused to expose her to such hideous sights, even though I didn't often succeed in keeping her off.

I am not exaggerating when I say that she seemed all too fond of studying corpses—almost the way she was with her beloved poisonous plants. She had no aversion whatsoever to blood, gaping wounds, or even ripped-out intestines, as I had to behold them just now. And she often found out what might have happened to a dead person, even if it were not as obvious as with the poor fellow lying in the dust in front of me.

I stood up and turned away. Fortunately I had not yet eaten breakfast, otherwise I might already have been on the run to the latrine to get rid of my stomach contents there.

In this case, Layla's special skills were not necessary. Any child would have recognized this unfortunate chap's cause of death. The lad had been bitten to death by one of the escaped predators that were just been driven back into their cages by Faustinius and his men.

I had recognized the mangled man when I'd bent over him. He was a slave of the ludus, one of the guards over whom Optimus had supervision. If I remembered correctly, he was called Livius.

XIV

When the last lion had been put back in his cage, I walked over to Optimus. I noticed that his left arm was bandaged, but otherwise he seemed fine.

"We'd already recaptured most of the beasts before you arrived," he told me by way of greeting. "I didn't want to bother your friend with it."

He pointed his head at Faustinius, who was routinely issuing orders to every available man and commanding his small team like a glorious centurion.

"But I am very grateful for his help," Optimus continued. "On our own, it probably would have taken us hours and we might have lost more men."

His gaze darted over to the corpse I had just inspected. With his brow furrowing deeply, he looked around, then leaned closer to me.

"Sabotage," he whispered. He murmured the word in my ear like a conspirator. "The beasts did not get free under their own power. None of the cages are damaged, I've already seen for myself. Someone must have unlocked them on purpose. And after that, they opened the gate that leads from the campus to the west wing of the ludus."

"Where Nemesis has her chamber?" I asked.

He nodded somberly.

"Was she seriously injured?"

"No, thankfully not."

Optimus narrowed his eyes, but I could still see how upset he was. At the same time he seemed rather proud, because as he now went on to tell me, it was he who had saved the life of the gladiatrix.

"Someone must have literally driven the beasts into her chamber," he explained to me. "She was asleep, of course, unable to defend herself in time with shield and sword against such a cowardly ambush."

"But you just happened to be around again and rushed to her aid?"

I hadn't intended to sound so cynical. What was it to me that Optimus had taken such a great liking to the gladiatrix that he wanted her protected at all hours? Although she was an extremely defensible woman.

He screwed up his face.

"I was just walking around for a bit because I couldn't manage to sleep," he defended himself. "There were others on guard duty tonight."

A question came to me that Optimus would not like. I asked him anyway: "Could it be that the gladiatrix herself released the animals—and simply did not expect how wildly they would rush out of the cages?" Driven as they were by hunger and anger, because they had been deprived of their freedom. "Perhaps Nemesis planned another assassination attempt, but quickly became the hunted herself and just managed to escape to her chamber, where you found her and rushed to her aid?"

Optimus' jaw muscles tightened. "And who is supposed to have been her intended victim in this attack?"

"One of the other gladiators? There are other quarters in the adjacent north wing, aren't there? Those of the free fighters. Maybe she was targeting one of them, trying to drive the beasts there."

Optimus remained polite, as was his way, but contradicted me most vehemently. "Why, by Jupiter, should she want to do that? She is not competing in any more fights during the current games. You know that. So why kill another gladiator in such a cowardly way?"

I didn't have an answer to that, except perhaps that the gladiatrix had systematically desired to kill every successful gladiator she'd encountered on her travels through the empire. Did this Amazon harbor a passionate hatred for men, which she gave vent to in this strange manner?

No, that sounded too crazy to be true.

"Maybe she just wanted to cause confusion and then flee the ludus unseen?" I made another attempt to explain. "Remember, she told us last night that she wanted to leave as soon as possible."

"Which you forbade her to do," Optimus replied.

"Rightly so, I think. After all, she's a murder suspect!"

"Releasing wild beasts as a diversion while risking your own neck seems to me a rather clumsy method for an escape attempt," Optimus remarked dryly.

I sighed, "You're right, my good man."

I stood there perplexed for a moment, then I addressed my friend again.

"Who was on guard duty last night?" I asked him. "In this part of the school—that poor guy lying half-mangled in the dust over there?"

I gestured with my head over to the remains of the slave I had just inspected earlier.

Optimus nodded wanly.

"I assume each gate is guarded at night?" I asked further. "But I don't suppose the beasts' cages are watched separately?"

"No, we thought the animals were safe in their cages," Optimus said. "There were several men on night duty. They don't stay in one particular spot, but wander around on patrol. Rusticus was in charge—the man I sent to you as a messenger this morning."

I nodded. By now I was well acquainted with the bearded fellow and his lofty brow.

"And Livius over there was probably patrolling the campus when the beasts got loose," Optimus continued. He pointed to the bloodied corpse still lying in the dust. "If he were still alive, he might be able to tell us how they escaped; who opened the cages and made the animals their deadly weapons."

"And Rusticus, or any of the others who were on duty last night, didn't notice anything before the beasts were released?" I asked further.

Optimus shook his head. "Rusticus swears he was properly on duty. He—and the men under him—noticed nothing suspicious, saw no one lurking about. Nothing. He swears that the gladiatrix must have put a spell on them. That she clouded the men's senses and therefore could get to the cages unseen."

"So Rusticus thinks she released the animals?"

"Yes. He and the majority of my men actually fear Nemesis as if she were an evil sorceress. Most of them have rather simple minds, I'm afraid. In truth, one or two of them were probably taking a nap, giving the assassin a clear path. I am sorry to say that discipline among my guards here at the ludus is not yet where I want it to be. I'm still working on that!"

He let out a growl that made me think of a wolf. I truly would not want to be a guard who got caught loafing by this man.

I looked up at the sky, which stretched above our heads in brilliant blue. The sun was already fairly high, and from the nearby streets the sounds of the awakening city reached my ears. Wheels rattled, mules brayed in their characteristic way, shopkeepers opened their stores. Life took its usual course. Only here, in the gladiator school of Varro, nothing was going as it should.

I decided to leave today's morning program of games to Marcellus and his co-sponsors. I would stay out of the VIP stand and turn the ludus upside down instead! No matter the cost.

My ambition as an investigator, a position to which I had appointed myself and Layla, commanded me to solve the murderous mystery that surrounded the gladiator school before yet another person lost his life.

I decided to send a messenger to the legate's palace, where Marcellus and Layla were probably just setting out on their way to the amphitheater—but as far as she was concerned, I would prefer to have her by my side here at the ludus.

Marcellus wouldn't like that, and two fewer guests in the VIP area certainly wouldn't make a good impression. But I trusted that my black sphinx would somehow change her lover's mind, and that she would much rather solve the murders at the school than spend another day watching the games.

All right, she was no longer *my* black sphinx, but Marcellus's, but she could wrap the proud Roman around her little finger just as she had done with me many times before.

I had one of the slaves of the ludus bring me a wax tablet, filled both inner sides with a message to Marcellus, and folded it shut again. Then I gave it back to the servant.

"Have a messenger take it to the legate's palace as soon as possible," I instructed him.

In my message, I briefly described the events of the night, the sabotage of the beast cages, and I asked Marcellus for permission to get to the bottom of it with Layla's help.

Since you, my friend, are the main sponsor of the games, I wrote, *it would damage your reputation if something really shady were going on here. Poisoned gladiators, weakened in battle, possibly accompanied by a manipulation of the bets that the arena-addicted people love to place....*

Having penned these hints, I left it at that. I myself did not believe that someone had murdered almost a dozen people, and apparently had not yet reached the end of their sinister plans, just to make big money in the betting.

But I had to provide Marcellus with the kind of bait that I hoped he would take.

XV

My plan had been crowned with success. Faster than I would have thought possible, one of the legate's wagons drove up in front of the school. Layla got out—by herself. Marcellus, as the main sponsor of the games, could not afford to stay away from the arena. Just as I had foreseen.

Layla wore a bright, white, softly-falling robe that contrasted dramatically with her dark skin. Over her shoulders lay a blood-red cloak, and her black hair was pinned up in a complicated Roman style. She was a sight to behold.

Smiling, she rushed to meet me—and first reported that Marcellus was not thrilled about having to spare us on the VIP stand this morning.

"I will make it up to him," she added when I asked her if the legate was very angry.

I bet you will, I thought to myself.

For a moment my imagination ran away with me about what she would do to her lover to reconcile him.

I put a stop to these thoughts before Layla could read what was going on in my face. She simply knew me too well.

Immediately, I proceeded to give her Optimus's account of the events of the previous night.

"An attack on Nemesis?" she said when I'd finished. "That must have been it, don't you think? Or is someone just trying to damage the school's reputation? A competitor of Varro's? But he doesn't have one, as far as I know. Not in this part of the province, anyway."

I shrugged; after all, I hadn't found a useful explanation either.

Layla ruled out my theory that the gladiatrix herself could have released the animals to make off in the ensuing chaos. "A woman as brave as Nemesis would never resort to such a feint," she explained to me.

We retired to one of the school's private reception rooms, which Varro had willingly made available to us. He'd calmed down a bit since the last beast had safely been put back in its cage. At least he didn't look now as if he had faced death itself. Full of shame over what had happened at his ludus, he was most eager to thank us for our support.

"Oh, you must solve these heinous crimes!" he repeated several times, like a pleading prayer. Thereupon he hurried away, leaving us alone.

Today's fights in the arena would hopefully pass without any further incidents. Otherwise it might really look bad for the future of the newly-established school. Sponsors invested a fortune in the games they hosted. They wanted to promote their reputation, not to be gossiped about by the people—saying that the gods might be angry with them and thus have afflicted them with a series of misfortunes.

Layla and I got into a discussion about who could be a suspect for each of the crimes at the ludus, and what strange motives might have driven them. But we were going in circles, and our thoughts were getting nowhere.

Suddenly, Optimus showed up. I expected him to tell us about the positive conclusion of the cleanup work—but I was to be mistaken once again.

He shook his head unwillingly before he began to speak. It was as if he himself could not believe what he now had to report to us yet again.

"We are truly cursed," he announced in a grim tone. "I have just been informed that Telephus is nowhere to be found. He must have managed to escape from his cell this morning, while the guards had to deal with the beasts breaking out."

"How is that possible? The slave gladiators are locked in their cells overnight, aren't they?" asked Layla.

Telephus was the axe fighter who had made such a boring spectacle against Hilarius yesterday. He was the famous arena hero who had entrenched himself in such a cowardly fashion behind his shield and played for time ... and now he had escaped from the gladiator school?

Optimus grudgingly replied: "Well, Telephus, while a slave fighter owned by Varro, is still an asset of our school, a veteran to whom we grant certain, well, privileges. While he occupies one of the small cells in the south wing, we do not keep him under lock and key at all times. He has been able to move freely within the ludus—and must have used the incident of the beasts to escape. In all the chaos, of course, no one paid attention to who was going where, or even to who was leaving the school. Everyone was too busy saving their own skin and recapturing the beasts."

"So it was Telephus who opened the cages?" I speculated. "To cause confusion and thus more easily disappear, unseen?"

Optimus nodded hesitantly. "Looks like it. I've already sent some men out to track him. He won't escape us!"

His jaw muscles stood out tautly. I almost thought I could hear him grinding his teeth.

"An escaped gladiator, that's a bad thing," he added. "These people know how to fight, especially in man-to-man combat. Even an experienced legionary can't stand up to that. We need to catch Telephus before he attacks or even kills someone."

And before the reputation of poor Varro and his ludus suffers any further damage, I added mentally.

I wondered for a moment why Optimus hadn't taken it upon himself to pursue the escapee. But I decided I already knew the answer.

Nemesis—he did not want to leave her unguarded in the school. Not because he thought she was guilty, but on the contrary, because he feared for her life and wanted to protect her.

If she were indeed not responsible for the poisonings at the ludus, the killer was still on the loose.

Was Telephus behind these vile deeds? Had he fled because his conscience was bothering him? Was he afraid that he would be exposed and executed?

XVI

"I want to talk to Nemesis," Layla said when we were alone again. "Let's hear what she has to say about the beasts' escape."

I had already thought the same thing, so I didn't object.

We found the gladiatrix alone at one of the tables in the dining room of the school, where she had a bowl of the grain porridge in front of her that was the staple of the gladiators. The fighters were fed with wheat, barley, beans and the like to make their muscles grow. Meat was rather rare. A popular mocking epithet for gladiators was "barley eater."

Similarly to Optimus, Nemesis had been treated by the medicus with some bandages—and she looked as if she would have liked to enter the arena again today to finish off an opponent with her sword.

"I was overcome in my sleep by several predatory cats," she reported—after initially being very unwilling to pay any attention to us at all.

"By the time Optimus showed up, I had already fought my way to the side gate, but you probably already know that." She screwed up her face. "And I don't care what you think. I had no intention of escaping through that gate, but it was the only way to get away from the beasts. They outnumbered me. If I'd had my sword handy, there'd be lion stew for lunch today."

She stared at the bowl in front of her and put down her spoon, as if she had just noticed how little she liked her meal.

When she raised her head again, she gave me a proud and at the same time challenging look.

It was the first time I'd heard that Optimus had met the gladiatrix near the side gate. Optimus himself had concealed this detail, and I'm sure he'd done so on purpose. He probably wanted to avoid our distrust of Nemesis deepening even more than it already had. The good man was apparently so enthralled by the gladiatrix that he didn't even take the truth seriously anymore. The Optimus I used to know had always done that without fail.

"Can it be that you have enemies in Vindobona?" Layla addressed the gladiatrix. She seemed to be thinking about something completely different from what was going through my head.

Nemesis took her time with the answer. I tried to read in her face whether Layla's question merely puzzled her or whether she was trying to hide something from us. But I was not sure what was going on in the woman's mind.

"I've never been to Vindobona before," she finally replied. "This is my first time here. So how could I have made enemies in this town?"

"But you might have encountered one of the gladiators elsewhere," I objected, "in a foreign ludus, at previous games? Perhaps a fighter you humiliated wants to take revenge on you. So perhaps he is trying to pin a few poisonings on you, and also seeks your own life as well?"

Even as I spoke the question, I began to ponder. Could what I had just assumed be possible at all?

To want to kill the gladiatrix was one thing, but to murder a few people just to be able to pin the bloody deeds on her? That seemed to me to be quite far-fetched.

Nemesis eyed me coldly. "If a gladiator is defeated by another in a fair contest, that is no humiliation. Unless his opponent is a woman, is that what are you trying to say? Because it is shameful to be defeated by such a weak creature in battle? Is that what you believe?"

She didn't give me time to answer. "Of course," she said, twisting the corners of her mouth into a disgusted grimace. "As far as that goes, you men are all the same."

"What school did you actually fight in before you bought your freedom?" interjected Layla. I guess she hadn't given up looking for enemies from Nemesis's past.

"In the famous ludus of Ravenna," the gladiatrix replied with her head held high.

Her gaze met Layla's with wonder and curiosity, as I had observed between the two women before.

I couldn't help but think once again how little I understood the gentle sex. Although, as a matter of fact, neither Layla nor the gladiatrix could suitably be described as 'gentle.'

"I sold myself to that school," Nemesis added. "I became a gladiatrix by choice. And when I'd fulfilled my contract, I continued my career as a free fighter."

"What was it that drove you to the arena?" Layla wondered.

I expected another proud reply, something to the effect that Nemesis sought glory and honor and wanted to compete with the bravest of men.

But she merely shrugged her shoulders.

"Does it need a reason?" she asked. "It just seemed like the appropriate life for me. I'd never had any ambitions to try my hand at being a wife or mother. So I had to make a living on my own, and I was no good as a servant. Or even prostitute, for that matter. The skill of my hands is limited to that of wielding a sword and shield."

That sounded plausible, of course, but still I suddenly had the impression that Nemesis was lying—or rather, that she was trying to hide something from us.

The explanation sounded somehow rehearsed, and at the same time the gladiatrix seemed seized by nervousness. She fiddled with her hair, which was flowing over her shoulders this morning. The gesture would have suited an insecure young girl, but not this otherwise tough fighter.

The sideways glance I caught from Layla confirmed my suspicions. I read astonishment in it, skepticism and mistrust. She too must have noticed how strangely Nemesis had reacted to her question.

Layla probed a little further. "And before you became a gladiatrix?" she wanted to know, "Where did you live then? Who was your family?"

The public knew almost nothing about Nemesis. Like many male fighters, she surrounded herself with an aura of mystery. This allowed the people to form their own opinions, to indulge in fantasies that were usually much more romantic than the true facts. As I've mentioned earlier, it was rumored that this fighter was the daughter of a noble house, perhaps even that she came from a senatorial family. A loftier origin was hardly possible in the Roman empire.

However, she clearly didn't feel like telling us any more

about her past.

"What's with all these questions?" she said curtly. "You wanted to know if I had enemies here in Vindobona or among the gladiators. If so, I certainly didn't make them in my youth, before I became a fighter."

With a jerk, she rose from her chair. "Are we done now?" She didn't wait for an answer, but simply left the room.

"Clearly this woman is not comfortable talking about her past," Layla said, putting the obvious into words.

XVII

Our next steps within the ludus led us to Atticus—or rather he was led to us. He had probably learned of our presence and wanted to share some new insights with us.

He met us just as we were about to leave the dining room. With a hand gesture, he told us to follow him a little way until we finally found ourselves in a narrow corridor, where we were all alone. What he had to say to us was obviously not meant for other ears.

"I told you yesterday that I had been able to secure some leftover food from the convicts' breakfast," he began, "remember?"

Both Layla and I answered in the affirmative.

"As I intended, I tested them for traces of poison. I fed small samples of it to some captured rats last night. And just now I fed another portion of it to a wolf that was injured when the beasts broke out. Since he was lame and no longer fit for the arena, I used him for my purposes."

"I take it he died?" I said. "And the rats, too?"

The medicus nodded. "And very quickly. To kill these animals, it takes a smaller dose than it would for a human. I'm sure I don't have to tell you that. But even so, judging from how quickly the poor creatures perished...."

He shook his head. "There was quite a large dose of poison involved! We can therefore be sure that the convicts were killed on purpose, even if they just served as human test subjects for our murderer. If the food had merely been spoiled somehow, the rats would probably have survived. And the wolf, too, at least for a while."

He looked around as if he still feared someone might overhear our conversation.

Then he continued, "I can't prove it, but I suspect that the two gladiators—Mevia and Nicanor—were given the same poison. Perhaps a somewhat smaller dose, compared to the convicts, but deadly nonetheless."

I nodded. None of what the medicus was telling us came as a surprise to me.

Layla said, "If it is all right with you, Atticus, we will take a closer look at the bodies. Maybe they can tell us something more about the poison, and the killer."

With this, she once again shocked the poor medic—as she had done yesterday when she had shown off her amazing knowledge of poisons to him. Women who wanted to look at corpses clearly did not fit into the man's world view.

"Of course," he hastened to reply after swallowing hard several times. "You'll find the dead in the back of the shed that's on the campus. We'll store them there until the end of the games, when we'll bury all the fallen at once. I'm sure you can manage on your own, can't you? My duties...."

He broke off and made a meaningful gesture that was probably meant to show what a busy man he was.

We let him go. I rather preferred to look at the dead alone, or only in Layla's presence. We were not allowed to trust anyone in this ludus, not even the friendly and so-competent-seeming medicus.

What if he had not had to test the poisoned food on any

unfortunate four-legged creatures to find poison in it? What if he had actually tampered with the food himself?

But why, by all the gods, should he have done that? What could motivate a medic to poison the condemned, or even some of the school's gladiators?

Even if Layla didn't like it, the only one who had a meaningful motive for these acts was Nemesis.

But I did not start a new discussion about it at the time.

We took the path through the school's courtyard, but we were not to reach the campus before our attention was diverted by another strange occurrence. The dead in the shed had to wait.

In fact, we had almost reached the training arena that occupied the back of the courtyard when Layla noticed a cloaked female figure under the arcades of the portico, on the inside of the north wing.

The lady—for that was what she was, as one could easily recognize from her expensive robes—seemed to be in a great hurry. Her step was determined, but she probably didn't want to be recognized by any inhabitants of the ludus. Still, I doubted that she had sneaked in. The gates of the school were well guarded.

She hadn't noticed us until now, but I hadn't managed to recognize her face either. She had pulled the hood of her light coat deep over her forehead.

Layla, however, suddenly murmured in my ear, "It's Petronella. The wife of Iulianus, the dentist."

"How do you know that?" I asked. The woman had still not turned toward us.

Layla gave me a smile.

"I guess a woman sees what clothes, what shoes another is wearing," she explained to me. "And since Iulianus is, after all, a co-sponsor of the Games, I've had several opportunities in recent weeks to admire his wife's exquisite wardrobe. The sandals she's wearing are studded with pearls, see?"

I had to squint my eyes to inspect the shoes. Petronella was walking along hurriedly—but just at that moment she peered over her shoulder like a thief in the night—and spotted us.

She stopped abruptly, looking undecided about what to do. Her joy at discovering familiar faces at the ludus seemed to be decidedly limited.

Layla didn't flinch back for long, but called out a friendly greeting to the woman, and indicated that we should deviate from our path to exchange a few words with her.

I was just as curious as Layla as to what a respectable Roman matron wanted in such a disreputable place as the gladiator school, so I quickly followed her.

Petronella looked embarrassed, but immediately had an explanation ready as to what had brought her here. She touched her forehead with one of her delicate white hands and put on an expression of suffering.

"Oh, I have such a terrible headache today," she lamented. "I didn't feel like watching the games at all. Neither did you two, I suppose?"

She smiled at us—or rather at Layla.

"And what brings you here to the ludus?" I asked, perhaps a little brusquely.

"Well, um, I figured I could do a little ... how do I put it?

A visit behind the scenes. Yeah, that's it. I wanted to see how the gladiators lived. We know so little about these brave men, don't we? What their daily lives are like, their training, their accommodations...."

With these words, she continued on her way. She clearly had more important things on her mind than having a casual chat with us.

We let her go, but I noticed that she walked almost to the end of the north wing and then disappeared inside the building. What I also noticed—much to my astonishment—was that she was apparently expected.

For, just as she entered the building, the figure of a young man appeared at the threshold. I could only catch a glimpse of him, but that was enough for me. It was Hilarius, the net fighter who had taken on Telephus yesterday afternoon.

What, by all the gods, did a lady of higher rank want with someone like that?

Layla, too, had recognized the gladiator. She seemed to already be one step further with her thoughts when she turned to me.

"I guess a headache is no real hindrance when it comes to a little tryst with such a paragon of masculinity," she muttered to herself, grinning.

"If Petronella ever truly had a headache," I replied. "It was probably just an excuse she gave to her husband. Apparently the good lady has her own ideas about what to do with a gladiator. Outside of the arena, that is. I guess she wants to play her own personal games with the young fellow."

Layla's grin widened. "That may explain why Iulianus,

her husband, wanted Hilarius dead yesterday, after the fight," she said.

Only now did I remember what the two co-sponsors of the games had whispered to Marcellus when it came time to decide whether Hilarius would live or die.

Cornix, the merchant, had been concerned about the high fees payable to Varro that would come due with Hilarius's demise.

However Iulianus, Petronella's husband, had wanted the retiarius dead, although he had fought so bravely. I wondered if there was a connection between his verdict and the attraction that the young gladiator apparently exerted for Petronella.

XVIII

At that moment, voices were raised behind us.

Did this ludus never rest? One got the feeling of being caught in a beehive. How could one investigate such a heinous series of murders when one was constantly being overtaken by new events?

I had been pondering whether Atticus, the medic, might himself be our poisoner when we had met Petronella. Now I would have liked to discuss with Layla whether the dentist's wife might somehow be involved in the murders, even though the idea seemed crazy to me. But there was no time for that, because with the babble of voices the next event to claim our attention had already announced itself.

I turned, looking toward the east wing where the commotion seemed to be coming from. Under the round arches leading to the main gate, the shouts of angry men could be heard. The voices were unfamiliar to me, but then a new one joined in that I immediately recognized: it belonged to Optimus.

"Good work, lads," I heard him say. He sounded satisfied, if not relieved.

My curiosity was aroused. The corpses in the shed would have to wait a little longer for us. But the dead were very patient; they would not run away from us.

This time Layla followed me as I walked purposefully toward the rounded archways. We had not yet reached them when the men pushed their way into the courtyard.

I recognized a few of the slaves who were guards at the school, men who were under the command of Optimus. Between them they were now dragging someone muscular into the courtyard. He was tied up and must have taken a beating. His body was covered with scratches and bruises, and there was even a bleeding wound on his forehead.

"That's Telephus," Layla called out to me, just as I recognized the gladiator myself.

So his escape had been in vain. He could not have gone far before Optimus's men had caught up with him and overpowered him. Bruised as he looked, he must have offered them fierce resistance, and his pursuers had had to use force to get him to return to the ludus.

Who could blame him? An escaped gladiator, much like a runaway slave, often faced a very harsh sentence, even sometimes death. Slave owners who were especially strict executed their entire household if one of their servants dared to run away. This extreme reaction was a profound deterrent as you can probably imagine.

But that would not happen here at the school. The gladiators were too valuable to let them die outside the arena.

At my second glance, two of the guards had also received a few minor injuries during their hunt for Telephus. I almost felt sorry for Atticus. Not only did he have to care for the many wounded animal fighters and gladiators every day due to the ongoing games, he now also had to take care of all the slaves and guards of the ludus who had been injured today alone.

First the breakout of the beasts, then the hunt for Telephus. What would come next? One really did begin to think that the gods were pursuing Varro's magnificent new gladiator school with their wrath.

The guards threw the bound man into the dust. Only then did they allow themselves to bend over, gasp for air and enjoy the praise of Optimus, which he bestowed upon them bountifully.

Only when Varro, the lanista, rushed from his rooms did they straighten up again and respectfully step aside.

What would the school owner decide, I wondered. What fate awaited Telephus? And what preoccupied me even more: what had moved the glorious veteran of the arena to seek his salvation in flight?

Varro did not seem interested in the latter question. He looked like a man who already had too many problems on his hands, and was loath to worry about the motives of an escaped gladiator.

Unflinchingly, he addressed Optimus: "Get him out of my sight! Put him in the cell, and cancel all his privileges. If he manages to escape again, the person responsible will pay for it with their head! I will not tolerate security breaches in my ludus, damn it."

His face was flushed red and a vein of anger was throbbing in his neck. Even his hair, usually pomaded to perfection, was in disarray. A shiny strand hung in his face and sparkled like a miniature dagger threatening to poke out one of his eyes.

Security breaches—what a fancy term, I thought to myself. Was the lanista just expressing himself that way because Layla and I, the friends of his main sponsor, were present?

I suspected that it was so.

But the fact that Varro had spared Telephus's life probably had other reasons behind it. Certainly the lanista felt a passionate desire to punish the gladiator—but he was also a good businessman, and that probably had priority in this case.

To execute Telephus would have meant a serious financial loss for the school. Varro must have invested a small fortune in order to buy the legendary axe fighter from the ludus of Carnuntum. He wanted to make money from Telephus and see him die in the arena in the end—for which he could charge the respective sponsor a hefty fee—and reap up to fifty times the amount he received for a fight without a death.

It was probably this calculation that had led Varro to pardon Telephus. And with this decision, the lanista considered the matter settled. He turned away abruptly and hurried back to the building.

The guards seized Telephus and dragged him toward the south wing, where the well-fortified cells for the slave gladiators were located.

He let out a groan, but offered no resistance. The guards would probably give him a good beating before they locked him up; after all, he had endangered their lives by escaping. He might be too valuable to fear execution, but the guards of the ludus were replaceable. Overseers who let gladiators escape were themselves halfway to the arena—*ad bestias*.

"Have Atticus look at his wounds," Optimus called after the men. "Get him over to the hospital first before you lock him up!"

If Varro wanted the gladiator to live and continue to

fight successfully, it was necessary to provide him with medical care as well. Even superficial, seemingly harmless wounds could become gangrenous and kill a man.

So maybe the axe fighter would be spared the revenge of the guard slaves after all?

"Can we question Telephus later, once the medicus is done with him?" I addressed Optimus. "We need to find out what drove him, why he tried to escape."

"And what he has to do with the murders at the school," Layla added.

I nodded in agreement.

Optimus raised no objections. "He's at your disposal as you please," he said curtly. "I'll let my men know."

Then he left.

XIX

We finally directed our steps to the campus of the ludus, where the corpse shed was located.

I almost expected that something would stop us again, that a bolt of lightning would strike from the sky at our feet, or a rift in the earth would open up in front of us.

But nothing of the sort happened. My mind was probably a little overheated by the incredible sequence of events I'd seen in the last few days and even hours. Apart from that, the midday sun was also burning down from the sky by now. It was clearly too hot for the time of year—another indication that the immortals were holding a grudge against us.

But in what way could Varro have made the gods his enemies? After all, gladiatorial games were also held for the glory of the immortals, not just the applause of earthly sponsors. So what could the gods possibly have against Varro's new school?

I just couldn't wrap my head around it, and so I didn't dwell on the thought. Who could fathom the will of the gods?

Instead, I slowed my steps a bit so that Layla could follow me, and together we finally reached the shed where the bodies were stored. An unmistakable stench emanating from the building made it clear that we were in the right place.

I pulled a handkerchief out of the pouch I wore on my belt and pressed it under my nose. Layla, however, did nothing of the sort; she just strode purposefully toward the door of the shed.

What can I say? Of course I let the piece of fabric disappear again immediately. I couldn't let a woman tell me that I was squeamish, could I?

I hurried past Layla, to open the door of the shed for her, but that was not necessary. At that moment it opened all by itself, as if by magic.

At second glance, of course, we saw this was not the case. Two men emerged from the dim light of the shed and stepped out into the open. They were both equipped with oil lamps, and one of them had just made a well-filled leather bag disappear into the satchel he was carrying.

I blinked as if I were the one who had just stepped out of the semi-darkness into the glaring light of the sun. I just couldn't believe my eyes.

One of the two I saw before me was Rusticus, the guard from the ludus. Seeing him here surprised me only slightly. Perhaps he was responsible for burying the dead whose remains were stored in the shed?

The other, however, was a respected citizen of Vindobona: none other than Cornix, the merchant, and Marcellus's co-sponsor at the games.

Both men seemed surprised, even startled, to catch sight of us.

But Cornix immediately brushed off his trepidation. He put on a friendly smile and greeted first me and then Layla.

"What a surprise to meet you both here," he said, as if we

were the oldest friends in the world.

"I could say the same to you," I replied. "I imagined you to be at the arena, watching the games you are so generously helping to fund."

The man's smile became even warmer and more confident.

"Oh, the executions at noon," he said with a nonchalant gesture, "if I'm honest, I don't like them at all. Apart from the fact that they are a bit smaller and less lavish than planned, given the, um, unfortunate events here at the ludus."

He pointed with his thumb to the shed from which he had just emerged. "And so I thought I could use the time to do another, somewhat less unpleasant task. Anything is better than having to watch that slaughter that excites the masses so sickeningly."

He patted Rusticus jovially on the shoulder and added, "And this capable fellow here was kind enough to help me."

The slave also looked bolder now, nodding in confirmation of the rich merchant's words.

"A task?" I repeated, uncomprehending. "In the corpse shed?"

Cornix took the bag out of his satchel again, which he had put in there just before. He opened it and let me look inside.

"Teeth!" exclaimed Layla.

Even she took a step back, whom otherwise hardly anything could surprise or even shock.

Cornix smiled again. "Well, what can I say—a precious commodity, isn't it? We the living have use for them, while the dead, after all, no longer do."

My confusion grew. Of course I knew that deceased people were often robbed of their teeth in order to make elaborate dentures for aged wealthy people. This was the very trade in which Iulianus had made his fortune. But what did Cornix have to do with it?

I didn't have to put the question into words; he seemed to be able to read it off my face.

"My friend Iulianus is a master of his craft," he explained to me. "But he is also—how shall I put it—quite a snob, I'm afraid."

He smiled winningly. "He leaves the supply of the raw material he needs to others—to me, specifically. He himself would not get his hands dirty in this way. He is too refined for that."

When I still didn't understand, he continued: "I deal in teeth, my friend, among other things. I supply Iulianus and plenty of other dentists all over our province with this coveted commodity. I procure the teeth from those who die of natural causes, but also from those who are sentenced to die, who can be found so abundantly in the amphitheaters of the empire. I also buy them from the poor, who voluntarily tear their biters from their jaws in order to turn them into money."

He paused, smiled again, exposing his own flawless teeth, and added, "If you want to be successful as a trader, you mustn't be squeamish. I'm sure you can confirm that, can't you, Thanar?"

He tied up the bag again and put it back into the satchel.

"Naturally, I couldn't pass up on all these dead," he concluded, pointing once more to the interior of the shed, which lay darkly behind him.

"And Rusticus was assisting you with the, um, extraction of the teeth?" asked Layla.

"That's right, my beautiful lady."

He sketched an elaborate bow that seemed rather ridiculous.

"Does Varro know you procure your raw material here, as you call it?" I asked further.

The words came out of my mouth rather more brusquely than I had intended. I had to restrain myself, even though I feared neither Cornix nor any other man in Vindobona. One shouldn't get on the wrong side of the most respected citizens of the area for no reason, even if one found their business methods repulsive.

"What do you care?" Cornix replied airily. He was still smiling, but by now it looked somewhat forced.

"The lanista has no objections," Rusticus announced stiffly.

Which could mean either that the two had actually asked Varro for permission, or that they simply had taken things into their own hands without much ado.

I suspected the latter. It was also clear to me that Varro would hardly refuse such a harmless favor to a sponsor like Cornix, even if he only learned of it after the fact. After all, he himself had no use for the teeth of the dead. Well, he could have made money out of them himself, but he probably hadn't thought of that yet.

Rusticus had probably collected a generous tip from Cornix to help him with the gruesome task.

"Perhaps we can do business sometime, Thanar," Cornix told me in parting. "I hear you maintain good contacts with fur traders from the north, and that you trade in top-notch quality."

I nodded. False modesty was not appropriate now.

"I have an interest in it," Cornix said. "I know buyers who will pay good prices." There it was again, that bright white smile.

At that moment, I would have liked to knock out one of his teeth. I don't know why; I really don't tend to behave aggressively.

"Let's talk about it when we get the chance," I said, but without any real enthusiasm.

Cornix seemed satisfied. "Now if you'll excuse me, I have to get back to the amphitheater. There's no way I'm going to miss this afternoon's fights."

We let the two men go. At least they hadn't asked us what business *we* had in the corpse shed.

On the other hand, I would not have hesitated to provide them with an explanation. It was no secret that there were several dastardly murders to be solved at the ludus.

For a crazy moment, I toyed with the thought of how far Cornix would go to procure his coveted raw material. Precious teeth—the life of a commoner did not count much for men like him.

But Cornix had no reason to have poisoned the convicts; they would have been executed anyway.

XX

When Layla and I finally entered the corpse shed, we were met with sultry heat and the sickening stench of decay.

In the small barracks it looked like the aftermath of a battlefield. We realized that not only the human corpses were stored here, but also the animal carcasses from the arena that had not yet been processed into food.

The meat of wolves or bears was not exactly considered an exotic delicacy for rich gourmets in our corner of the empire. The body of a giant snake, lying like a thick rope in a corner of the shed, had also been left untouched.

Presumably these remains would be distributed among the audience at the *sportulae*, the raffle on the last day of the games. The average arena-goer was happy to get meat on his plate, no matter which monster it might have once belonged to.

I heard Layla take a single deep breath, probably to calm herself. In view of the smell in here, however, she would have been better off not doing so.

In the next moment, she had already turned to those bodies so carelessly thrown away, which had once been living people.

I rushed to her side and stared down at the dead.

Need I mention that it was not easy for me to take a closer look?

Cornix and Rusticus had apparently dislocated the jaws

of some of them to get at the teeth, their coveted prey. Some of the corpses now stared back at us as if they had succumbed to a nameless terror. Gaping mouths opened before me, in which only those black rotten teeth that Cornix could not turn into money remained.

The sight was horrible, yet I could not tear myself away from it.

I recognized the man who had gone by the name of Mevia in life, that still-inexperienced gladiator whom Nemesis had defeated on the first day of the games.

He had suffered only minor injuries in the arena and had been pardoned by the audience, but that night he'd suddenly been carried off by death. The fight had not killed him, but instead insidious poison, and I no longer had any doubts about that—even if I could discover no special signs of it on the corpse. His toothless mouth was a gruesome sight that sent a cold shiver down my spine, though at the same time sweat was gathering on the back of my neck.

Next to Mevia lay Nicanor, the Victorious, as he had called himself. The name had not brought him luck.

Nicanor had collapsed in the sand of the arena during his fight against Nemesis, as if the hand of the gods had personally snatched him from life. He, too, had been the victim of a poison attack—but on his corpse I could not discover anything that would have proven this assumption, either.

Neither his lips nor his tongue were discolored in any telltale way, nor particularly bloated. At least not when one took into account that Cornix and Rusticus had just wreaked havoc in his jaw. The black hole that was his mouth now seemed to gape accusingly at me.

Next to the bodies of Mevia and Nicanor lay the remains of two other gladiators who had lost their lives at the games, followed by a pile of badly mangled corpses flung carelessly into the corner: those convicts who had been executed in the arena.

I avoided a closer sight of them so as to go easy on my already very tortured intestines. After all, these dead had not fallen victim to the murderer we were trying to expose.

In the opposite corner of the shed, the apparently intact bodies were stored.

"I guess these are the poisoned convicts who didn't make it to their execution in the amphitheater," I said to Layla.

She nodded. "The murder victims—along with Mevia and Nicanor."

She walked around the shed, looking first at the two dead gladiators we were interested in, then at the pile of outwardly-intact convicts.

In doing so, she behaved like a medicus inspecting living patients. She touched the dead without shyness, pushed their eyelids up and looked at the iris; she felt their skin, muscles and joints, and last but not least she even sniffed the lips of the men, as if she wanted to kiss those toothless mouths, those gaping black holes!

I had to turn away. I couldn't bear this spectacle. In moments like these, I wondered if I really was doing the right thing by encouraging Layla in her morbid tendencies, whether, by turning more and more to the dead—and their murderers—we would not end up losing our own humanity.

"Something is wrong here." Layla snapped me out of my

philosophical musings.

"You mean apart from the fact that they were murdered?" I replied—admittedly not very eloquently.

She actually forced herself to smile, in the midst of all this decay, surrounded by these smells that seemed to have gradually crept under my skin.

Would Layla and I also reek of death and decay as soon as we left this morgue? I looked longingly toward the door, through which a few rays of sunlight were streaming in.

"Are we done here?" I said to Layla.

I longed for fresh air, for the sun over my head, and to put as much distance as possible between us and these carcasses.

But Layla remained where she was. No, much worse: she was now beginning to rummage through the pile of corpses! She pushed bodies aside, staring into the bloodless faces, into the toothless mouths.

"Will you give me a hand, Thanar?" she prompted.

I hurried to her. Even though I longed to get out of here as quickly as possible, and the mere thought of touching the corpses made me want to throw up—I would not abandon Layla, never. Not even on the banks of the River of the Dead, on the threshold to the Underworld, the realm of Pluto. Although it felt more and more as if we were standing in that very place.

"What are you doing?" I asked her as I swallowed several times and then, in disgust, seized the legs of a dead man whose arms Layla had grabbed. With our combined strength, we heaved him aside, revealing another corpse beneath him. Layla also examined his face.

"Listen, dear," I began—this tender term still slipped off

my tongue occasionally, but fortunately no longer in the presence of Marcellus. Now I was probably using it to counter the disgust that had taken hold of me with something that was beautiful and tender, and that the stench of decay in the shed could not harm.

"Is it really necessary to do such an, um, intensive investigation?" I asked.

I tried to sound casually interested—and not like someone who was about to choke his guts out. "Even if these dead people could tell us by what poison they lost their lives, how would that help us in finding their murderer?"

Layla shook her head, barely noticeably, as she rolled another corpse aside. "That's not the point at all," she said.

"What, then?" I asked, perhaps a touch impatiently. *Can't we please finally get out of here?* I added in my head.

"Didn't you notice?" she said. "Atticus told us about seven poisoned convicts, didn't he?"

"Yes, that's right. Why?"

"Don't you see? There are only six lying here."

She pointed with her hand at the pile of dead bodies we had just fanned out so that each of their faces was clearly visible.

I counted, only needing one glance to do so. Layla was right: there were six dead people lying in front of us. And I also remembered now that Atticus had told us of seven.

"The medicus must have made a mistake," I said. "Or one of the bodies has been dumped somewhere else."

I looked around the shed again. But neither among the gladiators nor the animal carcasses could I spy a supernumerary human corpse.

I turned, barely able to hide my disgust, toward the heap

where the executed had been thrown.

But at that sight I had no doubts that every single one of them had indeed met their end in the arena. The corpses were charred, bitten, mutilated, and the list went on. None of these unfortunates had been poisoned. No convict who had died in the ludus had mistakenly ended up in that pile.

"That one more convict might have died at a later hour than the others, I could imagine," Layla said. "As the medicus has told us, the same poison may work faster on some, and much slower on others. So one more corpse wouldn't surprise me. But one *less*? And I already know who is missing, too."

XXI

I must have been staring at Layla like an apparition in the night, a ghost that had its abode here in this place of the dead. Or even Charon, the dark ferryman himself.

"Brigantius," she said. "He should have been executed yesterday at noon, with great spectaculum, but he was among the dead who were poisoned at the ludus. Now, however, I cannot discover his body anywhere."

"Brigantius?" I repeated incredulously. Of all people, the robber chief whom Layla and I had managed to capture?

We had hunted this villain for a long time, persistently, and had risked a lot to bring him down. I had been quite angry yesterday that he would not be executed in the arena. The people who'd suffered so long under him and his bandits had a right to see him die.

And now his body had disappeared into thin air?

I took a step closer to the pile of poisoned bodies that Layla and I had fanned out. I looked at each corpse again.

Layla was right; Brigantius was not among them.

"A misunderstanding," I muttered. "That must be what's going on here. Perhaps his execution was merely postponed, and he was not among those poisoned at all. Rusticus, who told me of his death, may have been mistaken. I'm sure Brigantius is safe and sound in his cell. And that would mean that he will die in the arena after all."

"And the medicus got the number of the dead wrong?"

asked Layla.

"Hmm. Must be that way. Do you have a better explanation?"

I turned toward the door. Any reason to finally get out of this shed was fine with me.

"Let's go," I said. "We must talk to Atticus. Surely he will clear everything up."

But he could not.

We found the medicus in his small hospital, where he was treating an animal fighter who must have been attacked by a bear that very morning. The wounded man gritted his teeth while Atticus poured a foul-smelling liquid over his half-torn arm.

Asked about the missing man in the corpse shed, the medicus stared at us as if we had just risen from the dead ourselves.

"Brigantius?" he said. "He was certainly among the dead. I remember seeing him when the slaves took him out of his cell. He was poisoned, just like the others."

"You examined him in detail?" I asked.

"Well, no—I really didn't have time for that yesterday. My duty is to the living, not the dead. I looked at three or four of the corpses to find out what might have taken them so suddenly, and I had the guards tell me how they died. As I told you, I suspected poison as the cause of death, but I didn't have time to look at each victim in detail. After all, these men were sentenced to death anyway, but they just found it a little faster, and outside of the amphitheater. They deprived the audience of a good spectacle, but hardly anyone will have to atone for their deaths, will they? And I'm a busy man," he added, as if he had to justify himself to us.

"It looks like one of those bodies wasn't really dead at all," I said, and Layla corroborated my words with a thoughtful nod. She was probably already pondering what the disappearance of Brigantius's body might mean.

The robber chief must have survived the poison attack at the school. I thought again of the words of the medicus: each person would have reacted differently to the same poison. The same dose could kill one, but might only cause violent nausea in the next.

Brigantius had probably been near death, unconscious, when he was found in his cell. Since so many others had been taken at the same time, none of the guards had taken a closer look. No one had bothered to check the man's pulse.

Yes, that's how it must have happened; they had mistakenly declared him dead.

Had the bandit regained consciousness many hours later, perhaps during the night, in the midst of a pile of corpses?

A gruesome awakening, but at the same time it had been a chance for him to escape his death sentence. The corpse shed was not locked—Brigantius would have been able to simply sneak out. After that, he would only have had to overcome one of the walls of the ludus unseen—which was probably not an impossible challenge for a notorious robber who was physically strong and used to life in the woods.

"Brigantius seized the opportunity," I said to Layla after

we had left the hospital. "Just as Telephus did, when he took advantage of the beasts' breakout."

"Marcellus will not be pleased to hear that Brigantius is now at large again," Layla said.

"The scoundrel will gather his remaining faithful around him and once again haunt the streets of our province," I confirmed with a sigh.

Frankly, I had little desire to go hunting for this bandit again. And as far as the poisonings at the ludus were concerned, we hadn't made any progress. Our honor as investigators and murder-hunters was at stake.

Not that anyone would have considered such an activity honorable, even if it were crowned with success. Least of all Marcellus, who would certainly have preferred his beloved to spend her time reading some poetry or the latest epic, or chatting with a few other Roman matrons in the legate's palace.

Layla and I decided to direct our steps toward Varro. I thirsted to know what had led Petronella, the wife of Iulianus, to the gladiator school this morning—or, more precisely, to the chamber of Hilarius.

I could of course have easily guessed what she wanted there. The question was rather: did the lanista know about this secret rendezvous? And could it have anything to do with the poisonings—with the beasts that had broken out—the escape of Telephus—the disappearance of Brigantius?

My head was spinning and felt hot, as if a wildfire were blazing there.

I just couldn't believe that there might be any connection between Petronella's tryst and the chaotic events at the ludus.

Layla, however, would not comment in either direction when I asked for her opinion. She merely wrinkled her dark forehead and once again looked like the famous sphinx.

XXII

At first, Varro pretended to be clueless. "Petronella, a guest at my school?" he asked in surprise.

"Petronella, a guest of one of the gladiators," I corrected him. "And do you mean to tell me that you don't know anything about that? Then I must assume the security at your ludus to indeed be in a dire state. If every gladiator does what he wants, receives guests, walks out the gate.... What's next? Do the fighters help themselves unhindered to the armory—and start a riot?"

"All right, all right!" Varro raised his hands defensively. "I know about Petronella's visit. She offered me a large sum for Hilarius's favors. And for my discretion! I sincerely hope I can count on yours, too, if we must talk about it? And I assure you that I will take drastic action. As far as security at the ludus goes, I mean. You—and your esteemed friend Marcellus—can rest assured that the city is in no danger from my school."

I nodded slowly, pretending to be halfway convinced. Then I assured him of our full discretion and asked again about Petronella's visit to the ludus.

Now he no longer dithered, merely rolled his eyes, then readily gave us the information: "Petronella had already approached me about Hilarius two or three weeks ago," he reported. "She'd observed him at a training fight some time before, when she had come to visit with Iulianus and

the other sponsors. They had a few of the gladiators perform in the training arena to make their selections for the
games. Hilarius was one of them. And Petronella wasn't in
his chamber for the first time today, if you must know."

He flashed a nervous smile. "After all, Hilarius is a handsome fellow, isn't he? And I'm sure I don't have to tell you
how much the gladiators are coveted by the womenfolk."

No, he really didn't have to. After all, even in his own
days as a gladiator, he had caught the eye of a rich widow.

"And Iulianus?" asked Layla. "Does he know what his
wife is up to while he's tending to the teeth of his illustrious clientele?"

"You bet! He's fully aware that she's a slut."

He fell abruptly silent, then bowed his head as if to apol-
ogize for his brusque words.

Immediately afterwards, however, he continued in an almost unchanged tone of voice: "Iulianus foretold it to
me—that his wife would come to the ludus on her own,
and that she would pay for one of my fighters, with his
own money."

"And he doesn't mind?" I asked in amazement.

Varro shrugged. "I don't think he cares what Petronella
does—or rather, with whom she's doing it. As long as no
one finds out about it, and his reputation is not jeopard-
ized. Iulianus himself, of course, does not offer her any
sort of conjugal love life. She is no longer young. And she
hasn't borne him any children yet, so he has long since
given up that hope as well. He will probably end up without an heir."

Varro ran his hand over his skull, probably to check
whether every single hair was still in the right place. "A

shame," he mumbled.

"And what about Iulianus himself?" asked Layla. Once again, she had put on an innocent air, one designed to mask her curiosity. She sounded like she was just making casual conversation.

But she did not deceive me. I saw the alert intelligence in her eyes, the determination to bring the truth to light. Even though—as I have already noted—I had my doubts that Petronella's nymphomaniac tendencies could have anything to do with the deaths at the ludus.

"Iulianus?" said Varro. "He didn't come to me to pay for the favors of a gladiator, if that's what you mean. Or the gladiatrix, which would probably be more to his liking. He probably has his own pleasure slaves at his house, reading his every wish from his eyes. Just like every other rich man, right?"

"Petronella definitely has it much worse," Layla muttered to herself.

I took my leave of Varro and motioned for her to follow me out into the open.

When we were standing again in the courtyard of the school, under the open sky, I said to her: "So this is why Iulianus did not want to pardon Hilarius yesterday, after his fight against Telephus. Our good dentist may know what his wife is up to, but he is probably not completely indifferent. He saw Hilarius as a competitor and wanted to take revenge on him, don't you think?"

"Looks like it," Layla said, "apparently he does begrudge Petronella her pleasure after all."

XXIII

The afternoon had long since arrived. I had not actually wanted to miss the gladiator fights announced for today, but first there was still another interrogation to be conducted at the ludus. Business before pleasure, as the saying goes.

Layla and I sought out the cell wing, where Telephus was now locked in one of the tiny chambers owing to his escape attempt.

The guard who was on duty—a fellow whose name I didn't know—didn't want to unlock the gladiator's cell for us, but he let us talk to him through the barred door, while he himself retreated to the other end of the corridor. He watched us from this vantage point with suspicious glances. Above all, he did not take his eyes off Layla; he must have wondered what a legate's mistress was doing in the cell block of a gladiator school.

At least we could talk to Telephus undisturbed. Or rather, we first had to convince the veteran to talk to us at all. He was leaning against the wall of his chamber as if turned to a pillar of salt and staring at the ceiling.

"I have nothing to say to you," he grumbled when we approached him.

"I think you do," I replied. "Tell us why you escaped. Are we to suppose that it was you who released the beasts? To continue your murderous work with them? That you did not yet have enough men on your conscience?"

He did not answer me, but merely eyed me in confusion.

"Don't tell me you didn't notice it," I continued. "A number of men have been murdered in the last few days, among them two brave gladiators like yourself. We want to find out who killed them, and I expect you to help us, to tell us everything you know in order to bring the culprit to the cross. Or to the arena," I added.

"I don't know anything," Telephus said lamely.

He looked like a broken man, no longer fearing anything, not even possible execution.

I noticed how he eyed Layla: she seemed to embarrass him, but not merely because of her beauty. It occurred to me then that he might be more likely to talk to me if she weren't there, that he didn't want to humiliate himself in front of her by revealing the real reason for his escape.

Even though I couldn't be sure if I was right in guessing this—I leaned over Layla's shoulder and asked her in a whisper to let me try talking to Telephus alone.

She immediately understood and quickly moved aside.

When her footsteps had faded away, I stepped closer to the iron bars and called out to the gladiator: "How is it now, Telephus? A man-to-man conversation? I give you my word that I'll keep anything you tell me to myself."

With a soft groan, the fighter detached himself from the wall against which he had been leaning and came to the bars. He examined me closely, his eyes marked by dark rings, his eyelids heavy.

"It was the gladiatrix who poisoned Mevia and Nicanor," he told me with a suddenly-awakened passion. "Good men, brave fighters, both of them. If you wish to atone for the cowardly deeds of this witch, I am your man. Tell me how I can help you."

"By telling me why you escaped from the ludus," I insisted.

"That has absolutely nothing to do with those dastardly assassinations," he retorted.

"Let me decide that, will you?"

His eyes narrowed to hostile slits.

We wouldn't get anywhere like this. I had to gain this man's trust before I could get a single word out of him.

"How long do you still have to serve with Varro?" I said, changing course. "Won't your time be up soon? After all, he bought your contract from the lanista of Carnuntum, didn't he?"

It took a moment for Telephus to come up with an answer, but at least he was talking to me now. "I still have two years to go—but we both know that I won't live to see the end of my contract."

"Oh? Are you doubting your abilities, a glorious veteran like yourself? Though I had not seen you fight before yesterday, I had heard only the best about you."

This was not flattery, but the truth. It was why I was so surprised that such a man had staged a cowardly escape from the school.

I expected him to revolt and defend himself passionately—but he merely shrugged his shoulders.

"I'm getting old," he said, "I guess that's it."

"Old?" I repeated. "What are you, thirty years? Thirty-five? Certainly not more."

I received no answer; the fellow really was a tough nut to crack. But somehow he touched me and aroused my pity.

It was as if a once-proud fighter had been beaten with red-hot irons, breaking his will forever.

"How many times have you fought?" I tried to keep the conversation going. "And how many times did you win? Fifty fights out of seventy, is that really true?"

Now there was a certain sparkle in the man's eyes. "Fifty-three victories, if I don't count the one yesterday. I'm not proud of that one. But even in the Flavian amphitheater in Rome I can claim four successes!"

The largest arena in the world. Only the best of the gladiators were allowed to fight there. The Roman audience was ultra-critical and incredibly spoiled.

I paid tribute to Telephus: "An incredible achievement. Few fighters can look back on such a career. You must have earned enormous amounts of prize money long ago. Surely you could buy your way out of Varro's school if you wanted to retire, instead of risking execution with an escape."

A melancholy smile suddenly played around the corners of the man's mouth. He grasped the bars with both hands and looked in the direction Layla had disappeared.

"She is the legate's beloved, is she not? But was once yours, I hear?" he said. "How did you get over her deception, so that you are seemingly still friends with her? It is beyond me."

What was this about? I really didn't want to talk about my love life or my—admittedly very complicated—relationship with Layla. Was Telephus up to no good after all, or what was he trying to achieve with this diversionary tactic?

"I don't expect an answer from you," he said after we'd

stared at each other in silence for a while. "Of course it's none of my business. I merely hoped to find understanding with you ... for a great stupidity I committed. In the ludus of Carnuntum, which you mentioned, I had indeed already saved the necessary sum to buy myself free. But I was so foolish as to give it to a girl I loved."

He broke off once more, but then he continued speaking more fluently: "She was fond of me too, or at least that's what I thought. She was a house slave at the school, and the lanista had it in for her. Every night he had her come to his chamber—and did abominable things to her. He was a man with deviant tastes, and I wanted to save my beloved from him. So I gave her my savings, which would have been enough to buy the freedom of half a dozen house slaves. They are not as expensive as an experienced gladiator," he added, modestly lowering his gaze. "But the lanista demanded an immense sum to give my beloved her freedom."

I nodded. I had fortunately never been in such dire straits, but I would also have given everything for the women I had loved in my life, although there had only been very few. My entire fortune, if that had been necessary. So it seemed I had not been mistaken about Telephus: he was a man of honor.

Suddenly he gave a throaty laugh. "Do you want to hear the end of the story? My sweetheart bought her freedom with the money I gave her, and the next day she was gone from the ludus, never to be seen again in Carnuntum—though she'd vowed to me that she would stay in town, close to me. That she would wait for me until my contract reached its end—and hopefully I'd be still alive. And then, just by chance, I found out that the lanista had demanded only a tenth of the sum for her release that she'd mentioned to me. She must have kept the rest of the money for herself. And I also learned the whole story—that she was the lanista's pleasure slave, whom he abused and tortured—had been nothing but a lie."

"She was just trying to cheat you out of your money?" I asked.

He nodded silently.

The poor man—what horrible deeds people were capable of! Even women who seemed most sweet.

Again we stood in silence for a moment, but now there was no longer any animosity between us.

When Telephus finally spoke up again, he said, "Optimus thinks highly of you. He says you're a just and honorable man, one to whom his friends are everything. And I trust in Optimus's judgment—one could use the same words to describe him, if you ask me. He treats those who are even at the bottom of the ludus with respect and dignity. He does not judge hastily, always has an open ear for our problems..."

"Why did you try to escape this morning, Telephus?" I asked into the silence that had arisen. "And why did you fight Hilarius yesterday like a rank beginner? Forgive me for speaking so bluntly, but that was exactly my impression. Never would I have thought that I was watching a celebrated veteran of the arena, considering how lamely you were swinging your axe against Hilarius and entrenching yourself behind your shield. Do you think you were poisoned, too? Did you feel yourself weakened? Was that the reason? Talk to me, man!"

Telephus averted his eyes and did not give me an answer.

For my part, I now grabbed the bars with both hands. He and I knew that I was putting my life at risk with this gesture. If he'd wanted to, he could've grabbed me and broken my neck with his bare hands. A seasoned gladiator like him, even with nothing but his fists, was a deadly weapon, and a damn fast one. My body would sink to the ground before I knew what had hit me.

I hoped that I was expressing my trust in him with this move, but he didn't really seem impressed.

I addressed him again: "I will believe you, Telephus, whatever you confide in me. If you tell me that you had nothing to do with the release of the beasts, I will accept that. Or with the poison attacks at the school, either. But I need to know what really happened; what's going on in this ludus, and how you might be involved in all the mayhem."

He closed his eyes, breathing heavily.

But then, opening his eyelids again, he nodded. "Very well, Thanar, you shall hear the truth. I won't be able to hide it much longer, anyway."

XXIV

With his head held high, he now sought my gaze.

"I have had nothing to do with the escaped beasts," he told me in a solemn tone. "Or with the poisonings at the ludus. I swear that to you on my honor. When the beasts were released, and chaos broke out, I merely seized the opportunity. I tried to flee for my life, because I...."

Again he broke off. His voice suddenly sounded as if he were strangely moved.

"I'm losing my sight!" he blurted out. He came close to the bars, which I had since let go of. "There, now you know!"

I almost let out an "Is that all?" But I was just able to restrain myself.

"Only at the edges of my vision," he added. "In the corners of my eyes. Or when I lower my gaze all the way down. But in battle, that's fatal! If I can't spot quickly enough what my opponent is up to ... I am doomed."

My gaze wandered to his eyes, which looked perfectly normal. But of course I could not seriously expect to recognize incipient blindness there.

Telephus carefully touched his eyelids with his fingertips.

"In everyday life, it's not a problem," he said. "Hasn't been until now, at least. When you stand here in front of me, I can make out every detail of your face. But in the arena, when things move in a blur, and my life depends on being able to grasp what's happening next to me, out of my immediate field of vision or at my feet, where a retiarius' net may be trying to bring me down...."

He shook his head. "It's been going on for a few fights, but yesterday was especially bad. And worse, where will things go from here?"

I stood there, embarrassed. I had expected the most outrageous explanation, but not this one. That a fellow in his prime, in full possession of his powers, would be struck by blindness like a helpless old man. Telephus did not seem to have any doubt that his visual impairment would only get worse in the future. Was he afraid that he would soon lose his sight completely?

What a cruel fate!

"Have you talked to the medicus about it yet?" I asked.

He laughed harshly. "What good is that going to do? No one can cure blindness or stop it when it creeps up on a man, afflicts him like a demon in the night. And if Varro learns that I am losing my sight, he will see to it that I die sooner rather than later. He will sacrifice me in a fight, against an opponent whom I would have easily defeated in the past, in order to collect the fee for my death from the sponsors—so that he gets back the money he invested in me. That's why I sought my salvation in flight, Thanar, because I am doomed to die, but I don't want to die yet! There is still strength in my limbs, still passion in my heart. I could even love a woman once more, trust her, have a family with her—and the home I never knew."

When I left the ludus with Layla a short time later to finally join Marcellus in the amphitheater, I relayed Telephus's words to her.

She listened to me in silence and nodded a few times at the appropriate points.

When I had finished, she said, "A very sad story, if it is true. And things will probably play out just as Telephus fears; either he will eventually succumb in the amphitheater, no matter how defensively he may fight—and then the public will not spare him, not even the once-glorious star of the arena. The memory of the masses is short. If he fights as disappointingly as he did yesterday against Hilarius..."

She shook her head. A strand came loose from her long black hair, which she had pinned up into a complicated style. I resisted the impulse to brush it behind her ear.

"Or ... what's the other alternative?" I asked instead.

"Or Varro will find out that Telephus' eyesight is fading. Then he will sacrifice his dearly-bought gladiator before he can mess up any further fights in the arena and thereby damage the school's reputation. Varro will deliberately pit him against an opponent who can defeat him."

"I thought to myself...." I began, but then hesitated for a moment.

Layla looked at me expectantly.

She stopped even though we had almost reached the amphitheater.

"Go on?" she asked. And the way she smiled, she seemed to have already guessed my answer.

"Well, I figured since I can't hire Optimus now, and I am definitely still in need of a capable guard for my house and transports..."

"...you could make Varro an offer for Telephus?" Layla completed my sentence, as she was so fond of doing.

I nodded.

"You'll have to pay a hefty price for him," she pointed out. "As long as Telephus's reputation is still excellent, Varro can collect a princely fee for him if he lets him die in the arena."

"I'm aware of that," I said. "And Varro is not going to give me a discount. He's an excellent businessman, I think."

"But...?" Layla asked. Her smile was even more evident now.

"But I'm not a poor man and I can afford it."

"Hiring a guard who may soon go blind?"

"Just because his eyesight is dimming doesn't mean he will go completely blind," I replied. "And if the worst comes to the worst, if I won't be able to use him as a guard anymore, he can still be a porter or a worker. He's not old yet, and he's very strong. Trustworthy too, I imagine. That's what counts most, isn't it?"

Layla took my arm while we walked the last few steps back toward the amphitheater. From the arena, wild screams from the audience reached our ears; apparently a gladiatorial fight was underway that was particularly worth seeing.

"You have a good heart, Thanar," Layla whispered to me as we took our seats behind the sponsors in the VIP stand.

They were all sitting in their opulent chairs: Marcellus, Cornix and Iulianus, and they were so engrossed in the fighting that they hardly noticed our arrival.

"Let's just hope Telephus doesn't turn out to be a

murderer in the end," I replied to Layla, trying to hide my embarrassment. "Who might have killed almost a dozen people, just to cause chaos in the ludus and escape."

While I was proud of my people skills and my insight into human nature, it wouldn't be the first time they'd let me down in a most painful way.

XXV

That evening I'd planned a guest banquet at my house, to which I had invited Marcellus and his gladiatorial games co-sponsors.

I had not been involved in hosting the games, nor had I been invited to the evening parties at the villas of Cornix or Iulianus, but for that very reason I insisted on entertaining them at my house.

Also present was Faustinius, my old friend the animal catcher, who was still staying with me as my guest. His wealth easily surpassed that of Cornix or Iulianus, but he did not boast about it, keeping modestly in the background tonight.

My house was located away from the city, north of the Danubius river, but over the years I had transformed it into a thoroughly splendid and very Roman country residence. With some satisfaction I registered the astonishment reflected in the faces of both Cornix and Iulianus as I led them through my atrium. Only recently I'd had one of the murals redesigned there so that it now showed a fight between a venator and two majestic leopards.

I entertained my guests in one of my triclinia, a dining room that I had furnished in the Roman style. Magnificent dining sofas made of fine woods were grouped around low tables. People lay or rather lounged together for the meal instead of making themselves comfortable on a bench or a chair.

Just as Cornix and Iulianus would have done at banquets in their villas, I provided a most varied menu. From fresh Danubius fish, game, baked dormice and fried eggs, to grilled pigeons and stuffed dates, I offered many things to please the most discerning gourmet's heart. And of course I also served sought-after wines, provided background music and had some acrobats, jokers and dancers perform for my guests.

It was to be a lavish celebration. After all, I—as a barbarian in Roman eyes—really did not want to be accused of offering hospitality that was inferior to that of the richer Romans and other citizens of Vindobona. My esteemed readers may forgive me this little vanity; my brother, a Germanic chieftain from whom I had been estranged for some time, would have unquestionably regarded my behavior as treason.

Iulianus had come without his wife. Petronella was indisposed, and very sorry that she could not accept my invitation, he told me.

"The good lady must be exhausted from wild sex with Hilarius," I secretly whispered to Layla.

Marcellus was engaged in an animated conversation with the other men, so Layla was able to leave the table briefly and join me in stretching my legs for a bit. A covered terrace overlooking the Danubius bordered the dining room where we were having dinner, and the evening breeze was almost as mild as a zephyr on a summer's day.

We stood under the round arches that led from the dining room to the outside, and gazed out at the moon-silvered water. How often we had done this before, when

Layla had still been living under my roof! We both loved the night sky, the lazily flowing waters of the great stream—and each other. At least that's what I'd thought back then.

But Layla seemed to shiver, so we returned to our sofas. Had it been just an excuse, because the river and the stars reminded her of our shared past in the same way that they filled me with nostalgia?

A flute player was just improvising a happy little tune for my guests as we made ourselves comfortable again at the table. A slave hurried over and filled our cups with deliciously cool honey wine. My ice cellar was still well stocked, despite the unusually warm spring, and provided drinks of a perfect temperature.

Layla followed the flutist's playing attentively. She probably liked the music very much, but nevertheless her thoughts seemed to be revolving incessantly around the games, and the murderous puzzle we had to solve at the ludus, just as mine were. The look on Layla's face as she pondered a seemingly unsolvable problem was almost as familiar to me as my own thoughts.

"Today the fights probably went well, to the satisfaction of the audience and the sponsors," she began, while looking in the direction of the men, who were engaged in an animated chat.

The conversation that Marcellus was having with his co-sponsors revolved around the games, while the murders were not mentioned with a single word. Since we had started eating, they had been talking of nothing but the fights, the animal hunts, and the creative executions that had been offered in the arena today.

Right now, Cornix was praising the exceptional quality of the beasts Faustinius had supplied for the games. Iulianus joined in, and immediately the men got into a discussion about the animal fights that Layla and I had missed that morning. There was talk of a venator named Atrox who had taken on three wild boars at once, and of a giant bull who had defeated a tiger from faraway Asia. Faustinius accepted this praise of his beasts with a modest smile.

Immediately afterward, the gladiator fights that had taken place this afternoon were debated and commented on. Varro had really gone all out to gratify his sponsors—and the people of Vindobona—trying to offer them such games as they'd never seen before in this corner of the province.

Personally, I had been most fascinated by the duel of two *andabatae* this afternoon—gladiators whose helmets had no visor slits, so they fought each other completely blind. The remaining senses of these men were so finely sharpened that they had performed almost as skillfully and unerringly as conventional gladiators. The defeated of the two had been pardoned at the end owing to the cheers of the masses.

Was this a possible future for Telephus, I wondered, if I could not buy him off Varro as I intended?

Cornix launched into an enthusiastic monologue about the battle of a *pontarius* against two *secutores*.

The pontarius was a net and trident fighter, like the retiarius, but fought—as his name suggested—on a small bridge. This was attacked from both sides by the secutores with their short swords and large rectangular shields.

This afternoon the pontarius had won a glorious victory.

The audience had raved with delight, and more than one lady had thrown kissing hands to the brave fighter and showered him with fiery declarations of love.

As I've said, the sponsors were satisfied. It seemed to me that they had long forgotten about the murders at the ludus, or that they really didn't give a damn about them. What did men like Cornix or Iulianus care about the lives of a few gladiators, or even convicts who were doomed to die anyway?

I myself listened with one ear to their animated conversation, but at the same time lost myself in thoughts of Alma. When would she finally arrive in Vindobona? How would it feel to have her at my side at banquets like this, beautiful and smart and kind, just as Layla was? The two women had become good friends, which only made everything all the easier.

Oh, I longed for her, but I didn't forget that I was once again in the middle of a murder investigation. I would not let her feel that; I'd devote as much time as possible to her, even though it didn't look like we would resolve the events in Varro's school any time soon, unfortunately.

XXVI

We had already moved on from eating to drinking, when a slave reported to me that a messenger stood at the gate. He came from Optimus, from the ludus of Varro, my lad told me—which caused me to rise immediately from my sofa and follow him with hurried steps into the atrium. There I received the messenger and listened to what he had to say.

"Optimus sent for you," he began.

I already knew that much, so I nodded impatiently. "What happened?" I asked. If Optimus had sent me a messenger at this late hour, it could not mean anything good. Had there been another murder at the school? Had the phantom we were hunting sabotaged something again, as he had done with the animal cages?

A rustling behind my back made me whirl around. Layla emerged from the darkness of the corridor I had just hurried down myself.

She had probably moved away from the table inconspicuously, driven as always by her insatiable curiosity. She joined me, eyeing the messenger with a questioning look.

I asked the man to continue. The poor fellow was still panting quite breathlessly; he must have been riding as if an army of demons were on his heels.

"The gladiatrix..." he gasped, "she has vanished from the ludus. But not departed, for her shield and chest are still in her chamber. Only her sword, it seems, has gone with her. Optimus has already sent out a search party for her, but asks for your assistance, and if it would be possible to ask your friend, the legate, for some legionaries? So that the gladiatrix can be tracked down quickly, despite the hour of night."

From the man's words, I could hear the great concern that must be on Optimus's mind. He probably thought the gladiatrix was in danger—instead of interpreting her disappearance as an escape. He was doing the thinking with his heart, not his head.

I myself did not know what to make of this latest incident. The fact that Nemesis had fled with only what she was wearing—that didn't fit. On the other hand, she would have had to take a wagon to carry her luggage, and such a vehicle was simply too slow for a clandestine disappearance. And too conspicuous. It needed good roads to get around. With a wagon, one could not simply vanish somewhere in the endless forests that surrounded Vindobona.

"An admission of her guilt?" Layla asked me. "Is that what you think?"

I couldn't bring myself to have an opinion. Neither in one direction nor the other.

"Let's find her," I said. "Then hopefully we'll find out what drove her."

I ran back to the dining room, signaling to Marcellus that I wanted to speak to him in private for a moment. Fortunately the other men were engaged in a conversation, most of which was being carried on by Faustinius. He was relating what sounded like episodes from his travels, which had taken him all over the empire and beyond. He was just describing how he and his men had captured crocodiles in the Nile. These huge monsters with their razor-sharp teeth had rarely been seen in an arena in the past, but lately they seemed to have become all the rage.

Cornix and Iulianus were listening spellbound to Faustinius' report, so I could detach Marcellus from them without causing too much of a stir. I took him aside and told him in a whisper about the disappearance of the gladiatrix.

"I knew it!" he exclaimed. "That witch poisoned her opponents! And now she steals away like a thief in the night, before we can charge her and she finds herself as a spectaculum in the arena at noon."

I did not enter into any discussion about the guilt or innocence of the gladiatrix, although the legate's words made sense, of course. I simply asked him to send a messenger to the camp to mobilize a few legionaries to search for the missing woman.

He readily agreed to my request. He himself would lead the men, he told me, and was already halfway out before I could stop him.

With a loud voice he demanded his horse, seemingly forgetting that he had come with Layla in the wagon. Moreover, in the course of the evening we had all partaken abundantly of the gifts of Bacchus, and were perhaps a little drunk. But we would probably manage the short ride to the ludus.

I instructed my men to saddle a horse for the legate, and one for me, of course.

Then I hurried back to the dining room once more and

asked Faustinius to stand in for me as host at the table. I was able to persuade Layla to stay under my roof for the night.

To my relief, she didn't insist on getting on a horse and accompanying us in our search for the gladiatrix. I would only have been mildly surprised had she come up with this idea.

However, she made me promise to inform her immediately by messenger when the missing woman was found.

XXVII

Within perhaps an hour Marcellus had gotten half a centuria of his men out of bed. The legionaries were ordered to first scour the area around the ludus and the amphitheater.

I myself joined Optimus, who began to roam the woods west of the school with a few of his men, but soon abandoned his venture.

An unmanageable network of narrow paths crisscrossed the forest, a labyrinth at night in which one inevitably got lost. If Nemesis had escaped this way, she would probably run astray herself, and in the end fall victim to a hungry pack of wolves.

Just as we'd decided to turn back, we heard a distant call. It was the voice of a man who seemed to be looking for Optimus. We heard him shout my friend's name several times.

We found our way to the fellow—it was a slave of the legion who had been sent out as a messenger.

From him we learned that the legionaries had managed to track down Nemesis. She was alive, but badly injured. We were expected as soon as possible south of the city, on the grave road, the place where the citizens of Vindobona buried their dead.

I couldn't help but notice the pained expression on Optimus's face at this news. He tried to get more details out of the messenger, but the man just shook his head. "I'm afraid that's all I was told, sir," he apologized.

We followed him without wasting any more time.

"Nemesis is supposed to have escaped along such a well-used road?" Optimus shouted at me as we hurried back towards town, together with the messenger. We had tackled the forest on foot as there was little advantage to be had on horseback. Because of the narrow paths and hanging branches, one would have had to constantly dismount and lead one's animal. It was not much more than a mile to the grave road from the clearing where we had met the messenger. So we set off on foot right away. To return to the ludus and have two horses saddled there would have taken even more time, if there were even any horses left in the stables at all. Every available guard from the school was out tracking the gladiatrix.

"At night, even the great Roman roads are deserted," I pointed out to Optimus. "Nemesis may have considered the southern road the best escape route. After all, you can make good progress on it. And perhaps she was hoping that her disappearance wouldn't be noticed at the ludus until morning."

Among the magnificent funerary monuments that lined the arterial roads outside every large city in the empire, there were at most a few cheap prostitutes hanging around after dark. And in addition to them, a dubious rabble that pursued questionable occupations. None would stand in the way of a fleeing gladiatrix; such people preferred to mind their own business.

Optimus didn't give me an answer.

We parted from the messenger who had found us and

sent him to my house, to keep my word to Layla. I had promised her that I would send her a message as soon as Nemesis was found.

I instructed the slave to tell Layla that we would take the gladiatrix back to the ludus by a direct route—thus I hoped to avoid having my fearless friend set out for the grave road. It really was no place for her, especially not at night.

When we finally reached the south of the city, we did not have to search long among the graves; a handful of legionaries met us at the foot of a magnificent tomb. It held the mortal remains of a wealthy horse trader and was adorned with stone horse heads. Its pointed gable towered into the night—competing with many similar mausoleums that crowded along the wide street.

Those who thought highly of themselves wanted to be buried as close to the city as possible, and saw to it that their monument was ornate and expensive-looking. Even in death, people were still concerned about their good reputation and wanted to make an impression on their neighbors.

Two motionless figures lay in the grass that was growing behind the tomb of the horse trader. One of them—around whom a good dozen legionaries were crowded—I recognized as being Nemesis, the gladiatrix. Marcellus stood over her and drilled her with questions—to which, however, she gave no answer.

The other figure—a man, as I thought I could tell from his physique—lay as if dead in the dark, a few steps away from the gladiatrix. Nobody seemed to care about him.

"Ah, there you are, my friend," Marcellus greeted me. A hint of pride was audible in his voice, to which he was well entitled. He and his legionaries had tracked Nemesis down in record time.

It wasn't until Optimus got down on his knees next to her and let out a startled gasp that I noticed she was covered in wounds, some of which were still bleeding. From the looks of it, the legionaries had already applied some makeshift bandages made of coarse robing cloth—but this woman needed to see a medicus, and quickly. Had this fact escaped my friend Marcellus, out of his sheer ambition to interrogate her right away?

I walked the short distance to the other lifeless figure.

"This is one of the slaves from the ludus," Marcellus told me even before I could bend over the man and identify him myself. "He's dead, and by the sword. The gladiatrix's, I would think."

"That's Rusticus," I exclaimed as I looked closely at the dead man. I recognized the black-haired fellow with his full beard and thinker's forehead, whom I had encountered several times before at the ludus or in the arena. He was the guard that had helped Cornix with his harvesting of teeth in the corpse shed.

Optimus raised his head and looked over at me. There was bitterness in his eyes, perhaps grief over the loss of one of his men. But he did not leave the gladiatrix's side, and his concern was for her, not for a dead man who was beyond help anyway.

Optimus pulled Nemesis to her feet, but she couldn't really stand. He clasped her waist and supported her entire weight with his strong arms.

She still did not utter a word, and seemed to be in severe pain. Her otherwise attractive face was distorted with agony, and her breath came in gasps.

I was able to persuade Marcellus to take her back to the ludus by the quickest route. A mounted soldier lent Optimus his horse; he swung himself into the saddle, took Nemesis in his arms and slammed his heels into the animal's flanks.

However, when the horse extended itself into a trot, the gladiatrix let out a pained cry, so that Optimus had to rein in the steed. The injured fighter could not be expected to ride at a faster pace.

The body of Rusticus was thrown carelessly over another horse. He too was to be transported back to the gladiator school.

XXVIII

Who among my gentle readers would be surprised to hear me report that Layla was already waiting for us at the ludus?

Marcellus merely greeted her with a cold look. He refrained from entering into a discussion about the fact that her presence in the gladiator school, in the middle of the night, was highly inappropriate.

The legate certainly didn't want to embarrass himself in front of his soldiers, but on the other hand he wasn't tyrant enough to order Layla around, as many other men did with their wives. After all, she was merely his mistress, not his wife. She could leave whenever she wanted, although in that case she would probably have created a powerful enemy. Did Marcellus sometimes fear that she might return to me if he restricted her freedom too much?

I suspected it—and didn't envy him the dilemmas Layla often used to get him into, with her so-impetuous manner. She was really anything but an ordinary woman. The word *obedience* wasn't even part of her vocabulary, even if her meek nature might have been misleading at first glance.

Atticus was already waiting for us in the hospital, with an assistant by his side. Rusticus's body landed carelessly on a trestle, where it could be looked at more closely later, while the medicus devoted himself entirely to the badly-wounded gladiatrix.

In the meantime she had lost consciousness, and was lying on the doctor's table like a dead woman. We surrounded her while the medicus went about tending to her wounds with practiced motions. Judging from his expression, he was not convinced that she would survive the night. She must have lost a lot of blood from her countless wounds.

Layla turned away, focusing her attention on the pile of blood-stained clothes that the doctor had cut from the gladiatrix's body and carelessly pushed aside. On top of it lay the Amazon's belt, to which a bulging purse of fine leather was attached. Layla set about unbuckling it. The fact that she wet her fingers with blood in the process did not seem to disgust her.

She peered into the bag.

"A considerable sum left here," she noted. "So Nemesis probably wasn't ambushed by bandits. There's no way they would have left such loot behind."

I addressed Marcellus: "Was anyone around when you found Nemesis?"

He shook his head, but did not take his eyes off the medicus's hands. The doctor's dexterity seemed to fascinate him.

"No, there wasn't a soul there," he said. "But I can't say my men proceeded very stealthily. We worked our way along the road, calling to each other to stay in touch, and also rummaged—possibly quite noisily—through the undergrowth on either side. If anyone was hanging around Nemesis and the dead guard, they probably would have heard us coming a mile away—and made a run for it in time."

He turned to me, looking me straight in the eye. "But the matter is clear, I'd say. The gladiatrix and this guard, they fought each other. And Nemesis kept the upper hand. We just have to figure out why they clashed. Was Rusticus single-handedly following her and trying to stop her—could he have been so tired of life?"

He looked around at Optimus, but the chief guard merely gave him a shrug.

"I can't imagine," said Optimus. "Rusticus was certainly no coward ... but he was no hero either. If he had tracked down Nemesis, I'm sure he would have been smart enough to organize reinforcements first before attacking her."

"Well, maybe she was the one who spotted him first, and noticed he was pursuing her," Marcellus said. "Then she slaughtered him before he could get reinforcements."

"But who could have beaten her up like that?" I objected.

The legate had no answer to that.

The medicus washed and sewed, applied bandages, and mixed a potion, which he painstakingly poured into the still-unconscious fighter's mouth. It was probably a brew intended to strengthen her, I assumed.

Again and again Atticus barked orders to his assistant. The lad brought instruments, tiny knives and clamps, bandages, and ingredients for the potion, sweating in the process as if he were toiling in the smithy of the divine Vulcanus.

"Look here, Thanar." I registered Layla's voice.

She sounded excited. Turning to her, I saw her pull a small piece of papyrus, folded several times, from the gladiatrix's purse. She unfolded the piece of paper, smoothing it out as best she could with the edge of her hand.

I could make out that it was a message, written in a clumsy hand, but in good Latin.

Layla began to read aloud, astonishing us so much with her words that even the medicus paused for a moment before turning to his patient with renewed zeal.

"I have proof of how you managed to kill your enemies," Layla read from the sheet. "If you do not want everyone to know about this, come to the grave road south of the camp suburb at the third hour of the night. About a quarter of a mile along the road you will find the tomb of a horse trader on your left. Expect me there with five hundred sesterces. In return, I will keep silent."

Layla lowered the papyrus. "A blackmail letter," she muttered.

"Five hundred sesterces?" I said, stunned.

That was a handsome sum. Even a famous gladiator had to fight several successful battles to save up that much. The average legionary in Vindobona earned at most two sesterces a day.

"There are no aurei in the purse, are there?" I asked Layla. It would have taken five of the precious gold Roman coins to arrive at a sum of five hundred sesterces.

Layla shook her head. "No. From the looks of it, Nemesis was going to meet her blackmailer with a sword. She probably wasn't going to give in to his demands."

The sword of the gladiatrix had still been in her hand when the legionaries had found her. However, there was no trace of a gold treasure. Had the one who had wounded the gladiatrix so badly managed to rob her after all? Had he only picked the precious coins from her pouch to mislead us? But why then had he left the blackmail letter on her body?

I pondered what it all might possibly mean.

"Did the blackmailer perhaps take the gold," I said to Layla, "after he ambushed the gladiatrix?"

"That's also a possibility," she replied, "but then why not make the whole pouch—including the letter—disappear? Then we could have believed that Nemesis had fallen victim to a couple of muggers, and would never have learned of this blackmailer's existence. And that would have been in his best interest, wouldn't it?"

"I guess the man doesn't fear persecution," Marcellus intervened. "He has merely brought down a woman who is a fraud and a murderess—which I knew long ago. He writes, after all, that he can prove how Nemesis defeated her enemies. That she obviously didn't fight fair."

He looked first to me, then at Layla, and immediately continued, "So it is clear that she is behind the deaths of Mevia and Nicanor. And probably also behind the mass deaths among the convicts. Do you need any more proof?"

Again he paused for a moment, then added: "The letter writer certainly didn't make empty accusations, otherwise the gladiatrix would not have gone to this meeting. She had to realize how dangerous it was; that she was possibly walking into an ambush. And yet she followed this man's instructions."

XXIX

The medicus fought tirelessly for the gladiatrix's life, even after Marcellus had declared her guilty of murder.

In the end, Atticus washed off the blood and told us that the gladiatrix's fate was now in the hands of the gods. He had done everything that was possible for a human being to do.

"She's strong," he said. "She can make it."

Marcellus had already returned to the camp with his legionaries. "If she comes to again, lock her in a cell," he had commanded before leaving. "We will find a punishment for her that will give the audience in the arena something to remember."

Layla had stayed with me, explaining to her lover that she still wanted to talk to the gladiatrix as soon as she woke up. Eternal optimist that she was, she trusted that the divine Nemesis would save from death the brave Amazon who fought in her honor. And that the gladiatrix would have a lot to tell us about her attacker, if she actually survived.

This time, Marcellus had expressed his displeasure with Layla's stubbornness quite bluntly. "I really don't know what you still want to do here," he had snapped at her before turning to leave. Then he had simply stormed off without any farewell greeting to either of us.

"You shouldn't push him to the limit," I murmured to

Layla when he'd gone. "He's still the most powerful man in town. If you fall out of favor with him...."

Her brow furrowed, but she was not ready to back down. "Nemesis is innocent, and I will prove it. She must not be executed!"

"If she ever opens her eyes again," I said. I was nowhere near as convinced of that as was my stubborn black sphinx.

However, in the end Layla turned out to be right once again—at least concerning the survival of the gladiatrix.

Not too long after Marcellus had left with his soldiers, Nemesis opened her eyes.

Optimus, who had been watching by her bedside, alerted us immediately, and we reconvened at Atticus's hospital right away.

In the meantime we had made ourselves comfortable on the benches in the school's dining room, and fortified ourselves with a few bites that the slaves of the ludus had quickly prepared for us.

Atticus had left his patient in the care of Optimus and joined us, completely exhausted. But he had refused to go to bed until it was clear whether Nemesis would survive the night. Either he took his calling as a medicus very seriously, or he too was a secret admirer of the brave gladiatrix.

Nemesis was resting in a small room adjacent to the hospital. When we entered the room, she looked at us at first as if she didn't know where she was and who stood around her.

Atticus had a fortifying soup brought to her, which he fed her himself as to a helpless infant.

Her spirits returned surprisingly quickly. In the end she took the spoon from the hand of the medicus and brought it—shakily but nevertheless accurately—to her mouth all by herself. At the same time, she seemed to remember what had happened that night among the graves along the south road.

The first explanation she gave us was obviously a lie. She had been attacked by a band of robbers, she claimed—without mentioning the presence of Rusticus or giving us any explanation as to what she'd been up to on the grave road at such a late hour—or why she had secretly slipped away from the ludus.

Obviously her senses were still confused, and she didn't really know what she was saying. She didn't seem to realize that with such ridiculous excuses she could very quickly get herself crucified, if Marcellus found out about them.

Even Optimus, so obviously inflamed with passion for Nemesis, didn't buy her explanation.

"A gang of robbers, you say? And they left you your purse—and your freedom? Instead of carrying you off and selling you to a slave trader for a hefty sum?"

"I guess they thought I was ... dead," Nemesis replied. She still found it difficult to speak.

"Can't all this wait until tomorrow?" Atticus implored us. "Why don't you give her time to get her strength back? Otherwise all my work will have been for nothing in the end."

But Nemesis seemed eager now to defend herself.

"The bastards who attacked me weren't out to kidnap me," she explained to us, "they wanted to kill me! And they probably thought they had achieved their goal."

"And they almost did! Or they will if you don't give yourself strict rest!" Atticus intervened again.

Nemesis forced a smile. "You have done well, medicus," she said, "I thank you—and will reward you generously for your efforts."

"That's not what I've been about!" the man exclaimed.

At least he fell silent after that, shifting to the role of a listener and letting the gladiatrix have her way.

She continued, breathing heavily, but now in a somewhat firmer voice: "I even think I recognized the leader of the villains; it was one of the convicts from the ludus. I actually thought he was among the poisoned ... but apparently I was mistaken."

"Brigantius?" Layla exclaimed before I could say anything myself. "The robber chief?"

"That's the one," Nemesis said. "I'm pretty sure it was he who led the gang."

Her claims made no sense at all.

While I was still trying to make a connection between the escaped robber and the gladiatrix, Layla was already formulating the next question. Or rather, it was a request that she addressed to the gladiatrix.

"You should tell us the truth if you want us to believe you. What were you doing outside the ludus at this late hour? On the grave road?"

The Amazon's eyes darted back and forth a few times, wandering over the faces that were bent over her. Over the worried, yet skeptical face of Optimus, over the angry face of the doctor, who looked at his stubborn patient like an unruly child, and finally over my features and those of Layla. We both returned her gaze expectantly.

"I received a letter this afternoon. It was left for me at the gate," she finally said after taking a few deep breaths.

She was staring at the ceiling now, seeming not to want to meet either of our gazes. "After reading the letter, I ran to the gate and inquired after the messenger. But I was told that it was just some street urchin. It was hopeless to track him down, or even to find out who had sent him."

"Anyone who doesn't have their own slave handy to run errands makes use of these boys," Layla said, nodding. "No one pays attention to them or even memorizes their faces. They're too unreliable for verbal messages. But they are good for delivering a letter in exchange for a few coins."

So far so good. The words of the gladiatrix were going in the right direction. We had found the letter with her—and Nemesis had to know that. After all, she had carried the letter in her pouch, and she had to assume that we'd look in there to find out if she had been robbed.

"What did the letter say?" asked Layla.

Nemesis hesitated—a moment too long.

Then she said, "*I know who poisoned your opponents,* was written on the sheet. Then it named the place where I should come. The southern grave road, the horse trader's grave. And that I should bring money to pay the informant. A ludicrous sum of money. I took my sword instead."

"Oh, please!" I cried, "What a brazen lie! Don't you realize that we found the letter long ago, in your pouch—that we know its true contents?"

She looked at me uncomprehendingly.

For a moment I feared that her consciousness had clouded over, that she was close to fainting again.

But that was not the case. The conversation undoubtedly had upset her quite a lot, and she was obviously in pain from her wounds, but she bore it bravely.

A little color had returned to her cheeks, and her dark eyes were now sparkling at me with her fighting spirit.

Layla unfolded the papyrus we had found in Nemesis's pouch and wordlessly held it under the gladiatrix's eyes.

Nemesis skimmed the lines. She wanted to say something, but was suddenly seized by a coughing fit. She winced, gasped and moaned.

But then she started to speak again: "I've never seen that letter before! It must have been slipped to me when I was already defeated. And the claim is a lie! I fight justly and honorably, just like any male gladiator. I use no tricks that anyone could expose."

"I don't think the letter writer meant tricks," I said. "He wasn't writing about how you defeated your opponents, but how you *killed* them! He was referring to the poison that was proven to have been administered to Mevia and Nicanor, as well as the half dozen convicts murdered at the ludus. And he wrote of *enemies,* not adversaries. Which suggests that you harbored a personal hatred for your two victims. Am I not correct?"

She coughed again. By now, the blush of anger was visible all over her face.

"Calm down!" Atticus thundered. "Can we all just calm the hell down! Or you are going to kill her!"

He pushed himself protectively between us and his patient, waving his arms in front of my nose as if he wanted to scare away a few blood-sucking insects.

Layla took the floor. Her voice sounded soft and completely relaxed. I had no idea how she did it.

"So you're saying this isn't the letter you received this afternoon?" she asked the gladiatrix, pointing to the sheet of papyrus she was still holding in her hands.

Nemesis tried to shake her head, but immediately refrained from doing so. Every movement seemed to cause her pain.

"No," she moaned. "The letter that was brought to me had the wording I told you of; it spoke of exposing the poisoner. That was the only reason I went to the meeting. I wanted to finally clear myself of the suspicion you have against me!"

"And where is this letter now?" Layla continued.

"I burned it. In the little brazier that stands in my chamber."

All the better gladiatorial quarters in the ludus were equipped with such heating basins. The simpler cells lacked this luxury. Only the dining room and the training hall were kept warm by means of underfloor heating in the winter.

"And Rusticus?" I probed. "How did he get involved? Did you kill him because he was following you and trying to stop you from escaping?"

"I wasn't on the run, I just explained that to you! And I didn't see Rusticus at the graves, nor did I kill him!"

"However, he died by a sword that must have been very similar to yours in size and shape," the medicus interposed. "I've had a look at his body in the meantime."

The gladiatrix took a deep breath, was about to retort,

but then changed her mind.

She turned her head away and muttered, barely audibly, "You wouldn't believe a word I say anyway." And with that she fell silent.

I tried to ask her a few more questions, but she pretended I wasn't even there.

XXX

We left the small chamber. Optimus placed one of his men as a guard in front of the door, although the gladiatrix could hardly have escaped in her condition.

We asked the medicus to let us have a look at the corpse of Rusticus ourselves. The doctor was dog-tired and seemed to be barely able to stand on his feet, but he still wanted to accompany us to the main room of his hospital.

"I think we can manage on our own," I told him. "You go lie down and get some well-deserved sleep."

The man nodded gratefully and shuffled away.

Optimus, Layla and I directed our steps toward the central room of the small hospital—even though I must confess that by now I myself was longing for my bed with great fervor.

Rusticus's corpse looked exactly as Atticus had described it: a sword wound that would be a match for Nemesis's weapon gaped a hand's breadth below his heart.

However, his body was otherwise unharmed. It did not look like he had defended himself, or even fought a prolonged battle against anyone.

Optimus took the floor. "Do you think he tried to blackmail Nemesis? And that she killed him instead of paying him for his silence?"

"Looks like it," I said. "After all, we already know that the good Rusticus was very open to earning extras. He did help

Cornix break out the teeth of the dead, for example."

"But did he actually know what he claimed in the letter?" replied Optimus. "In the one we found in Nemesis's pouch, I mean. The other letter she claims to have received, I think she made up, didn't she?"

He looked at me questioningly, probably hoping that I would dispel the suspicion against the gladiatrix. But I did nothing of the sort.

"Nemesis may have killed Rusticus," I said, "with no problem at all. Even if she really is a fraud and not as outstanding a gladiatrix as she would have us believe. Rusticus wasn't a trained fighter, was he, Optimus?"

He just inclined his head.

"But who wounded Nemesis so badly?" interjected Layla. "Not Rusticus, surely? There's no way he could've done that to the gladiatrix without suffering even the slightest wound himself. Except for the fatal sword thrust."

"Not even if she's half the fighter she appears to be," Optimus confirmed.

"And this letter," Layla continued. "There's something wrong with it. Think about it: if the gladiatrix actually received the note we found on her; if she carried it with her, in her pouch ... then, when she came to in the hospital, she had to assume that we'd discovered it and read every single word. So why would she claim the content to be completely different, instead of coming up with a better excuse? It just doesn't fit."

"She was weakened," I objected. "Probably not in possession of her full mental faculties."

But this objection did not convince Layla. She shook her head. "No, I rather believe that they only slipped her this letter after she'd already been defeated. We were supposed to find it on her, so we would think she was our killer. Also, I'm sure that Nemesis actually did fight several men, just as she described to us, and not just an inexperienced slave like Rusticus. He would never have been able to beat her up like that."

"Let's go to her chamber," I suggested. "If she really burned a letter there, as she claims, then maybe the ashes of it are still left. Then we'll know..."

I hesitated. Know what, actually?

Would the remains of a letter really be proof of the gladiatrix's innocence? Or was this woman just a skillful manipulator playing her wicked game with all of us?

I didn't know what to think anymore. And Optimus— yes, and even Layla—seemed to feel the same way.

We went to the gladiatrix's chamber. There her chest still stood, where she kept her money and other valuable possessions. Nemesis had won many battles in her career. That was a fact, notwithstanding whatever means she might have used to do so. She certainly was in possession of a much larger fortune than she'd carry with her when she traveled.

Her shield was leaning against the wall. A few items of clothing were scattered over the bed and the lid of the chest.

In the brazier that stood in the corner of the room, we actually found ash residue—yes, Fortuna was kind to us, and we were able to even rescue a piece of intact papyrus from the black-gray dust.

The little scrap was barely bigger than my thumbnail, but there were still some letters visible on it.

"*Meme*—" I read. It was all that was left.

"*Memento*, maybe, or something like that?" suggested Optimus. "*Remember*, or *think of*.... That would fit into a blackmail letter quite nicely, wouldn't it?"

"Granted, but what did the letter writer want to remind her of? What was she being blackmailed with—if not the murders she may have committed here at the ludus? And, damn it all, who was it who wrote this letter? Was it Rusticus?"

"Nemesis claims the letter was delivered to her by messenger," Layla said. "So maybe it was written by someone outside the school, who used a street urchin to disguise his identity."

"Sending it by messenger could be a ruse," I replied. "Don't you think? Rusticus could have paid a boy to make Nemesis believe just that: that the blackmailer was not a member of the ludus."

I had the feeling that we were now going in circles and simply getting nowhere, lost in this hideous web of lies and the never-ending succession of incidents at the school—where you no longer knew who was the victim and who was the perpetrator.

"Was Rusticus even literate?" I asked, turning to Optimus with a flash of inspiration.

Unfortunately he confirmed that, yes, Rusticus had known how to read and write, although that was far from a given for a slave at a ludus. "That spidery scrawl of the letter we found on Nemesis ... that could well be Rusticus's handwriting. He read passably, but didn't write often," Optimus said.

"The content of that other—the *real*—letter must have

been highly sensitive in any case," Layla said. She pointed her hand at the brazier. "That's why Nemesis burned it immediately after she read it."

"Which again speaks against the woman's innocence," I said. "She clearly has something to hide, and the blackmailer will have figured that out."

Layla tilted her head. "She certainly seems to be keeping a secret, one that she's willing to put her life on the line for. And one that has been revealed to someone, whether inside the ludus or outside. No, inside the school, I'm sure of it. Because the murders could not have been committed by a stranger, an outsider."

I hesitantly agreed with her, and she continued: "That's why Nemesis destroyed the letter—and she went to the night meeting, knowing full well that it might be an ambush. She took the risk because she had no other choice. Someone took the opportunity to attack her. He left her dying, and if we hadn't found her so quickly...."

She broke off and turned to Optimus with a jerk. "You'll have to keep a close eye on her, around the clock. If Nemesis is innocent, she has an enemy here at the ludus who wants to frame her for his crimes—these countless murders—and who wants her dead. He will not rest until he completes his work. He made a mistake on the grave road by not ensuring that she had passed, but that won't happen a second time. And Nemesis cannot defend herself now, weakened as she is."

Optimus's eyes widened.

"Have her guarded, around the clock," Layla continued in the same forceful tone. "And only by men you trust unconditionally."

XXXI

The next morning I returned to the gladiator school to take a closer look at Rusticus's chamber.

I did not send for Layla this time, even though she probably would have liked to accompany me. I didn't want to strain her relationship with Marcellus any further. Or mine, if I were always inciting his mistress to further snooping.

Before we'd parted last night, Layla had announced to me that she wanted to talk to Nemesis in private. Today, during the day, as soon as the opportunity presented itself.

Which I took to mean: as soon as Layla could get away from the arena, where the fourth day of the games had begun. I guessed it would be around noon, when Marcellus might approve of her disappearing from the VIP stand once again. He himself would possibly have lunch together with Cornix and Iulianus, even though he liked to watch the executions.

A woman-to-woman conversation, then, between Layla and the Amazon; it would be an exaggeration to say that the two had become friends, but nevertheless there was something between them. A kind of invisible bond, if I may express it poetically. One woman, living far outside the norms, customs, and demure boundaries of her gender, recognized and respected the other, who did likewise, albeit in a different way. Nemesis fought and killed, while

Layla's passion was to expose murderers. Not the same, but somehow similar.

Would Nemesis confide to my black sphinx the secret she was hiding? And would this knowledge help us to finally solve the murders in the ludus?

I sincerely hoped so. But in the meantime, as I mentioned, I wanted to subject Rusticus's chamber to a thorough inspection.

The slave quarters in the school did not resemble a prison, like those of the unfree gladiators, but they were hardly more spacious. Rusticus had been a relatively high-ranking slave, one of the guards of the ludus. The house servants, menials and arena slaves did not even have their own chambers, but lived and slept in a common room, as was the norm on most country estates or even in magnificent villas.

Rusticus's tiny chamber, which contained only a narrow cot and a chest, was meticulously tidy. The man had apparently loved to keep it clean and neat. There was nothing to indicate that he had been dragged from his bed or attacked in any way in this room.

I rummaged through his chest, but found no large sum of money there, that might hint at some kind of criminal activity on his part or an already lengthy career as a blackmailer.

Next, I took care of the bedstead, but it was so shabby that there was hardly anything to hide in it—or under it. I pulled aside the coarse woolen blanket and lifted the thin straw mattress, but apart from a fat spider that had long since passed away, I found absolutely nothing.

I did not discover one item linking Rusticus to the

poisonings at the school or that could enable him to blackmail Nemesis. There was no telltale piece of evidence for which she would have paid a lot of money. Was it possible that the gladiatrix had removed it from Rusticus's chamber by now?

Not really, I answered myself.

Nemesis would certainly not have met Rusticus last night on the grave road if she had already exposed him as her blackmailer beforehand. A woman like her would have made short work of anyone who dared to threaten her, right here at the school.

Even though the gladiatrix may have lied about the true events on the grave road, it seemed plausible to me that she had not known who her blackmailer was.

And after we'd brought her back—half dead—to the school, she had hardly been physically able even to leave her bed. Let alone sneak into Rusticus's chamber to remove any traces or telltale objects here.

Optimus appeared behind me and entered the chamber, which made it a damn tight fit.

He must have been informed that I had returned to the ludus. By now the guards at the gate let me enter the school without having me state my name or my business first.

I told him about my unsuccessful search of the room. He merely nodded, having probably already checked everything himself.

He looked as if he had not been able to sleep during the whole of the previous night. Deep, dark circles surrounded his eyes.

I didn't ask him if he himself had kept watch outside the

gladiatrix's chamber, but I suspected as much. Probably there were not many men in the ludus whom he still trusted, after all that had happened.

I reached the arena, where the animal fights of the morning were still going on.

As inconspicuously as possible, I took my place in the second row of seats in the VIP stand. Layla was already there, and apparently Petronella did not have another tryst with Hilarius today either. The stout matron was dressed like the poshest women in the capital, wearing a silky, shimmering blue robe and earrings of gold and precious stones that must have cost a fortune.

She nodded at me as if she were greeting some menial she didn't care for. I felt an urgent need to ask her how Hilarius was doing today, and to do so in such a loud voice that everyone on the gallery would be able to hear it.

I resisted the impulse. Why was I so irritable? I was certainly not a quarrelsome man under normal circumstances. Was it this murder case that was getting to me?

I suspected so. Until now, I had truly not distinguished myself as an outstanding investigator in this matter.

When I next looked up, the sun was burning down hotly from the sky, and preparations were already being made in the arena for the noon executions. I had lost myself completely in thought, going over in my memory every incident in the ludus that might somehow be connected with the murders.

But still I had no clue, both as far as the identity of perpetrator was concerned, as well as the motive that might be driving him. I was completely in the dark. It was only a small comfort to me that Layla seemed to be no better off.

Cornix the merchant turned to me, his slightly reddish hair shimmering like copper in the midday sun.

"I heard about another death at the school," he began. He looked rather bored, but his voice was filled with unconcealed sensationalism. "And the gladiatrix is said to be responsible for it again, is that true? One of my grooms brought the news to me this morning on my way to the arena. These fellows, after all, are always well-informed about the latest gossip—so I must assume he spoke the truth? Yes?"

He eyed me as if hoping to read the answer from my face.

"Rusticus is the one who was killed," I replied. "Your assistant in the collection of the teeth." I mentioned it deliberately—and I hadn't spoken in a whisper.

Marcellus and Iulianus should be informed about the deeds of the oh-so-honorable businessman, always eager to flaunt his wealth and sophistication.

I can't say that I haven't done some pretty shady business in my own career as a trader, but those days were in the past now. And I had never presented myself to the outside world as slickly as this guy. At least that's what I hoped. There was not much left of my initial sympathy for the man. With some people, it was better not to make their closer acquaintance. Sometimes you didn't find anything beautiful when you looked behind certain facades.

Marcellus was looking questioningly at Cornix, I noted with satisfaction. He had probably not been aware of the tooth-collecting business.

Iulianus the dentist, on the other hand, didn't bat an eye.

Apparently he knew the sources of the teeth Cornix regularly sold him. He didn't seem to mind a bit, didn't comment on my statement with a word or even a raised eyebrow.

Instead, he turned to Marcellus. "Why don't you finally have this gladiatrix executed? That's within your power, isn't it?"

Bloodlust resonated in his words. The man suddenly reminded me of a hungry animal that was already licking its chops in the face of a sumptuous meal.

"I would so love to see that witch again in the sands of the arena," he continued. "Condemned *ad bestias*. What a fight that would be!" He ran his tongue over his brittle lips and looked at Marcellus with an expression of supreme pleasure.

What a disgusting person! Cornix was harmless by comparison. No wonder Iulianus's wife preferred the arms of a gladiator to the marital bedchamber.

"The legate will not execute anyone until their guilt is sufficiently proven," I replied with some passion. The look I gave first to Iulianus, then to Cornix, was probably not very friendly.

But so what? I did not depend on the friendship of these men. It also had its advantages, if one was a barbarian who lived somewhat apart from the city. And the two men disgusted me, each in his own way. It was the only reason I had taken sides with the gladiatrix. I was far from convinced of her innocence.

Marcellus gave me a dark look. He himself probably had no doubts about the gladiatrix's guilt. Nevertheless, he confirmed my heated words.

"That's right," he announced to his two co-sponsors. "No one will be fed to the beasts in my presence who is not proven guilty of a crime beyond any doubt. This isn't a country of savages, after all."

He gave me another look, which was not exactly friendly either. But at least he had spoken of *savages* and avoided the word *barbarian.* Clearly a concession to our friendship.

I was satisfied with that.

XXXII

Immediately afterwards, Cornix and Iulianus withdrew from the VIP stand to enjoy lunch away from the arena. This time, Petronella accompanied her husband.

Layla mumbled an excuse about needing to visit the ludus for an hour or two, and disappeared as well.

It was as I had expected. If everything went according to plan, she would have the predicted woman-to-woman conversation with Nemesis, and perhaps she would learn something of what the gladiatrix had kept from us until now.

Marcellus remained in his seat, and I stepped to his side to join him. Just like the common public, we ate a few sausages from one of the merchants who roamed between the rows of seats with their vendor's trays.

"What is Layla trying to accomplish at the school?" he asked me. "Shouldn't you at least be with her so she doesn't put herself in danger?"

I assured him that she would certainly not be in danger at the ludus in broad daylight. I knew Optimus to be on site, and he would never allow any harm to come to her.

"She wants to get the truth out of Nemesis," I added, to prove to my friend that we were actively working to solve the murders, not just blindly believing the gladiatrix's protestations of innocence.

He ate the last of his sausage and then cleaned his lips

with his handkerchief.

"If you ask me, you are wasting your time with this woman. Who but she would have the slightest motive to kill her opponents? And now Rusticus, too? Isn't it obvious what was going on? He must have known something, made some observation that could have been Nemesis's undoing—and he was fool enough to try to blackmail her with it. That's why she killed him off. I really don't know where there's any doubt left."

I nodded, not objecting. "Let's wait and see what Layla can accomplish," I said.

Marcellus's gaze wandered over the rows of spectators, then down into the arena, where a prisoner had just been dragged from the subterranean vaults up into the sunlight. There were separate elevators, operated by mules and slaves, which allowed people and animals to emerge from underground in this way. A dramatic sight, I thought; as if the underworld were rising up to spit out a few cursed souls.

"Do me a favor, Thanar, and return to the ludus. I want you by Layla's side when she confronts this Amazon. I my-self must..."

He halted, pointing with his outstretched hand into the circle of the arena. "My place is here. If I pay yet another visit to the school, gossip will only get worse. Surely you understand that."

"Of course," I said quickly, and rose immediately.

I was not sad to miss the executions, and I also under-stood the legate's concerns. He had invested a fortune in hosting these games. They were designed to enhance his prestige, which was very important for a man of his class and position. Constantly hanging around in such a disreputable place as a gladiator school was out of the question. It was bad enough that his mistress was being seen there again and again.

Marcellus was really a great man, that he allowed this to happen at all, I thought. That he—despite his original protests—was now watching Layla chasing after murderers together with me, trying to solve crimes.

Now it was just a matter of not failing at our mission.

Hastily, I left the arena and directed my steps toward the ludus, which already seemed as familiar as my own house.

Optimus received me personally at the gate. "Layla is with Nemesis," he explained to me without being asked. "She wanted to talk to her alone."

Varro the lanista rushed over as Optimus and I entered the courtyard of the school. He had just been busy giving final instructions to some gladiators. They were about to leave for the amphitheater, accompanied by their guards and helpers.

"Once again fate brings you to my ludus, Thanar," he greeted me sadly. "I cannot believe that we have been struck by yet another calamity. What have I done to incur such wrath from the gods?"

He looked at me with a puzzled expression, the corners of his mouth drooping like wilted vegetables, and his skin sallow. He appeared to have aged years during the last few days. Not even his pomaded hair seemed to shine today.

"Things are going well in the arena," I tried to comfort him. "Well, since yesterday, anyway. The audience is happy, and so are the sponsors."

He managed a weak smile. "Thank you for your

kindness," he said, then turned back to his fighters.

I exchanged a few words with Optimus to pass the time while we waited for Layla. At least the morning at the school had gone by without any new incidents, as he'd informed me.

When Layla finally emerged, she appeared glum and lost in thought.

Optimus began asking her questions, trying to learn what she had gotten out of Nemesis.

But Layla shook her head. "I promised her I wouldn't share what she confided in me with anyone," she said.

Optimus nodded, but his face was distorted. Curiosity and understanding struggled within him for the upper hand, as could be seen from his facial expressions.

"At least tell me if she was able to clear herself of the suspicion she's under?" he probed Layla.

She shot him a sympathetic look, but to my astonishment she didn't give him an answer. What might the gladiatrix have told her?

Layla had repeatedly expressed doubts over the course of the last few days that Nemesis was our killer—and now she was unwilling to proclaim the gladiatrix's innocence to Optimus?

I asked him to leave us alone, and thought about where I could talk to Layla in peace. Would she be as reserved with me as she was with Optimus?

We crossed the west wing of the school and entered the campus. Many of the animal cages here were already empty. The games were nearing their end—tomorrow was the last day—and thus the majority of the beasts had already lost their lives.

My eyes fell on two magnificent leopards sitting vigilantly in the tiny cages, growling at us as we passed them. I was struck with a sudden melancholy at the thought that their beautiful and powerful bodies would very soon lie perished in the sands of the arena. I was really in a most strange mood.

We walked a little further until we approached the shed where the dead were stored, men and animals together. The former were not only deprived of their lives, but also of their teeth. I felt as if the entire campus had turned into a burial ground, a forecourt to the underworld, where lost souls wandered in agony.

I desperately needed to pull myself together. I was not a lost soul; I had merely come here to this open area of the school with Layla to make sure we wouldn't be overheard. That was all.

I looked at her expectantly and she immediately understood what I wanted from her.

"It wasn't easy to get Nemesis to talk," she began, "and the story she finally confided in me under the seal of utmost secrecy is a very personal one."

"It's okay, I understand," I said. "You can't talk to me about it."

However, she shook her head. "I promised her that I would keep her secret, but I also told her that I must take you into my confidence if I am to help her, if she doesn't want to end up on the cross or at the stake. Because I'm sure that what she revealed to me—her past—plays a role, here and now, in the murders in this ludus."

A sound of surprise crossed my lips.

Layla smiled gently. "I think I was able to convince her that we're both on her side, that we want to save her life, to make sure she's not executed despite her innocence."

I had to think of Iulianus, of the man's eagerness to have the gladiatrix torn to pieces by wild animals, and to feast on the spectacle. Even though I was far from being convinced of the Amazon's innocence, everything in me resisted handing her over to the bloodthirstiness of such men.

"So you do think she's innocent, then?" I asked Layla. "Why didn't you tell Optimus that?"

She furrowed her darkly shining brow. "Because I don't want him to fall even more hopelessly in love with Nemesis. I don't think she's a murderer, but she's still a woman full of dark secrets, full of pain—and contempt for the entire male gender. As much as I would like it, I can't imagine a happy future together for the two of them."

"I guess that's true," I replied.

Then, however, I fell silent and waited attentively for the report that Layla was about to give.

XXXIII

"The story they're telling about Nemesis's origins," Layla began, "she's been spreading herself, to distract from the truth. She is not the daughter of a nobleman or even a senator; she was born the child of a slave. And as a young girl she had already been sold into the household of a rich Roman, serving as a maid in the man's estate in Baiae, where he used to stay only during the summer months."

Baiae was the luxury summer resort of the most distinguished Romans. It was located a few days' journey south of the capital.

Originally the small town in the bay of Neapolis had been famous for its healing springs, but nowadays it was a place that the more prudish philosophers reviled as a refuge of vice, indulgence and orgies. In short, a destination that many dreamed of, but where very few could afford to stay.

"Not bad," I said. "One can truly do worse as a slave. Leisure time for three quarters of the year, when the master of the house is staying in Rome ... and a life free from hard work in a luxury household."

I hesitated for a moment. "Her master treated her well, didn't he?" I inquired. I hadn't expected that Layla would tell me a nice story about young Nemesis's happy past.

"Well," she replied, "he was not a brute, and he did not make Nemesis—who was then called Delia—do heavy work. But he claimed her as a love servant, even at a very tender age."

I nodded wordlessly. It was a very common fate of young, beautiful slave girls. And before she had turned into Nemesis, the tough, relentless Amazon, the girl Delia might have fit the classical ideal of beauty. The gladiatrix she had become was still very attractive now, even if she seemed wild and untamed as a lioness.

"Her master demanded deviant things of the young Delia?" I speculated. "At night in his bedchamber?"

Layla shook her head. "He did not, himself—but he used to offer Delia's services to his male guests as well. And so it happened one night that Delia was already asleep when a visitor appeared in her chamber. She could barely recognize his face, only saw that he had dark eyes when the clouds outside the window briefly broke open and some moonlight fell into the room. His build was rather average; he was no giant. But he fell upon Delia with the brutality of a hungry beast. He—"

Layla faltered, and her voice broke.

I could see in her eyes how much this story affected her. She had once been a slave herself, a beautiful girl perhaps not unlike the young Delia, except for the difference in skin color.

I myself had never done violence to her when she'd been in my possession, but she didn't like to talk about how her previous masters had treated her, and I did not urge her to remember.

"No need to tell me," I said to her quietly. "I can well imagine what that fiend did to the girl. I don't need to know the details."

She nodded, furtively wiping a tear from the corner of her eye.

Then suddenly a wild smile flitted across Layla's face. "You know, little Delia was not as defenseless as her tormentor might have suspected. She endured the rape, knowing that she could not stand against the much stronger man in open combat. But then, as he rolled off her body, exhausted by his lust and with sleep overtaking him, she took her revenge. She had no weapon with her, but she used her teeth. With all her might, she bit into his manhood. She bit it off, Thanar! And then she ran. Ran for her life. She flew from the mansion, into the wilderness, where she hid from the henchmen they sent after her."

I sucked in a startled breath. "*Bitten off?*" I repeated incredulously. A sudden pain jolted through my loins, at the very idea!

"The man must have died miserably," I said. "Bled to death. Just what he deserved!"

"You would think so, yes. But Delia, who first found a hiding place with a peasant family very close to Baiae, learned a few weeks later that her tormentor had survived. Her former master, of course, had kept secret the terrible incident in his house, but the assistant of a medicus spread the story among the slaves in the area. The man in question—Delia never learned his name—had survived thanks to the outstanding skills of the doctor. He was forever deprived of his manhood, but managed to escape death."

"It's a miracle he didn't bleed to death," I said.

Of course, in a place like Baiae, where the villas of the super-rich crowded, the best doctors were available, but still....

A hardly bearable vision forced itself upon me. How a man near death had had a medicus seal the violently bleeding stump of his manhood with hot irons just to save his life. The unbearable pain, the stench of burnt flesh. And yet the man had deserved this fate, or even worse, if he'd done such violence to a young girl, as Layla had indicated to me.

To have fun with a pleasure slave was one thing; to treat her roughly and brutally, even to inflict serious injuries on her, was quite another. Even if every master was allowed by law to treat his slaves in any way he pleased—it was not acceptable. A behavior that was not worthy of a human being, in my opinion.

"And then what happened to Delia?" I wanted to know.

"She vowed to never again be defenseless and at the mercy of a man. She soon left the kind-hearted peasants, who could not hide a runaway slave forever, and struck out into the wilderness, learning to survive there. And to fight. When she finally returned to live among humans, she had become Nemesis. She didn't want to dwell in the darkness of the woods like a wild animal forever, but as a runaway slave there weren't many options open to her. She had to go to a place where no questions would be asked about a person's origins. A brothel was out of the question. A gladiator school, on the other hand, seemed suitable, because she loved the fight, sought the challenge, longed for the power that a masterfully wielded sword was able to bestow. She enrolled in a ludus that accepted women and took the sacramentum."

"The gladiators' oath," I said, "by which they vow to their lanista to be beaten, bound, and burned, even killed. As their new master commands."

Layla nodded. "Nemesis took it in stride, in exchange for being turned into a deadly weapon. Being shaped into a fighter who could take on any male gladiator."

She paused, looking over at the arches of the amphitheater that rose into the sky behind the walls of the school. "Nemesis didn't tell me any details about her training, but she must have worked on herself with superhuman toughness to become what she is now."

"An avenger?" I said.

I paused for a moment, then added: "Doesn't this story, this fate the girl Delia suffered, speak to the fact that she has now grown up to be a man-killer? A nemesis, as her name suggests. A messenger of the goddess of vengeance."

"The story isn't finished yet," Layla said. "Even though Nemesis—or Delia—assumed for many years that she had put her past behind her forever, that she would never have to remember what happened that dreadful night."

Layla raised her head, checking the position of the sun. "Shall we return to the amphitheater?" she said. "I think Marcellus—well, he'll be expecting us, won't he?"

She smiled uncertainly. It was obvious that she appreciated the amazing patience her lover was showing her, on the one hand, and didn't want to strain it, on the other. "On the way I'll tell you how Nemesis's past caught up with her. Here, of all places, in the school of Vindobona."

XXXIV

We had the guard at the back gate of the campus unlock it for us and left the ludus on the small path leading from there back to the street. The walk through the school would have been shorter, but Layla didn't want to risk us being overheard.

As we followed the path, she continued her report: "Nemesis did indeed receive a blackmail letter yesterday afternoon," she said, "but not the one we found in her pouch. According to her, this second letter was a ruse, planted on her just to make her look even more guilty and to finally pin those murders on her, which she didn't commit."

I skeptically raised a brow. "So what did the blackmailer write to her?"

Layla stopped. She furrowed her brows, as she often did when she wanted to concentrate on something.

Her voice took on a changed tone, as she quoted from memory, "Remember Baiae! The time of revenge has come. If you don't want everyone to know who you really are, come at the third hour of the night with five hundred sesterces ... and so on. This was followed by the description of the tomb where she was then waylaid. She carried no gold with her, but rather her sword. She did not intend to pay the blackmailer. But neither did she expect to be ambushed by a whole horde."

"The band of robbers? So that's the version of events she's sticking with?"

Layla nodded. "Only, the reason why she rushed to the meeting was different from what she told us. And she didn't understand for the life of her how anyone in Vindobona could know about the events in Baiae. She wanted at all costs to avoid being exposed as a runaway slave who had tried to kill one of her master's guests. I don't have to tell you what the penalty would be. Nemesis would end up where so many men would like to see her: in the arena, not with her sword in her hand, but as the highlight of the noon program."

"*Revenge for Baiae*," I mused. "That would have to mean, after all, that the fiend whose manhood she once bit off has tracked her down, here in Vindobona. But how in the world could he have succeeded?"

"I don't think he was chasing her. And Nemesis doesn't think so either. Probably fate just brought them together in this place by chance, and the man recognized her. After all, he knew what his host's slave girl looked like, the one he'd raped that night in Baiae. Before the fateful night he must have noticed her around the house, where she sparked his lust. While Nemesis has no idea what he looks like, especially not after so many years."

I nodded hesitantly.

"The red mark on her neck, you noticed that, didn't you?" continued Layla. "It looks like a lightning strike scorched her skin."

I nodded. "What is it? An injury inflicted by her tormentor?"

"No. She was born with the mark. But you can recognize

her from that, can't you? No matter how much time may have passed. Time in which the young, innocent Delia became Nemesis, the indomitable Amazon. Because of that mark, her rapist may have remembered Delia when he so unexpectedly met her again at the ludus. And the opportunity for revenge, which he had certainly not hoped for any more after all these years, suddenly came within reach."

I shook my head and slowly started moving again. Layla walked beside me.

"This is madness," I said. "Are we now to believe that this fiend, this castrato, killed nearly a dozen people—two gladiators, six convicts, the poor fellow who died when the beasts broke out, and then Rusticus? Just to pin these crimes on his hated enemy? Why not just murder her?"

"I don't understand that either," Layla admitted.

"But you still believe that the story Nemesis told you is true?"

"I do. You didn't see how she spoke to me. How much the young girl's dread and pain were still present, in the fearless Amazon who sat before me. She certainly didn't make up her torment."

Suddenly an idea came to me that made me stop again.

"Couldn't Brigantius, our escaped robber chief, be Delia's tormentor?" I exclaimed excitedly. "He may have moved in better circles in his younger days. Or he may have merely slipped into Baiae under a false identity as the guest of the gentleman who then owned Delia? Either way, his age would fit. He must have been a grown man by the time she reached puberty. Plus, Nemesis claims that she was assaulted by him and his henchmen, last night at that meeting place on the grave road."

"I've already asked her the same thing," Layla said, to my disappointment. Apparently, my idea wasn't that brilliant after all.

"And she said no?" I asked.

"You do remember what Brigantius looks like. He's a little older than Nemesis, that would fit, but his eyes..."

"Are of a bright blue color," I completed her sentence. "While Nemesis remembers that her rapist had dark eyes."

Layla nodded.

"Couldn't she have made a mistake? I mean, it's so long ago. In the moonlight, while she was being raped. Her perception may not have been reliable then."

"It's possible," Layla said.

"Hmm. But of course, any number of other men would come to mind, wouldn't they? There's no telling what kind of guests this former master of Delia's used to receive in his villa. Was he a Roman nobleman who moved only in the best circles, or an upstart, a new rich, who might also count shadier fellows among his friends?"

"The latter, according to Nemesis," Layla said.

"Which doesn't exactly narrow down the pool of possible candidates," I muttered. "That castrato could be one of the gladiators here at the ludus. A couple of them are of the right age. Or even Varro himself? One of Marcellus's friends? Cornix? Iulianus? Both men are older than Nemesis. We don't know how much older the guy was, do we? She only saw his eyes, not that he was, for example, elderly at the time?"

"He was not aged, he was a man in the prime of life, vigorous and—"

She hesitated, then cleared her throat. "And potent. Before Delia took her revenge on him, anyway."

"Alright." I raised my hands. "That doesn't really get us anywhere, I'm afraid. "We could, of course, order the slave gladiators of the ludus to present their private parts to us. But to explain the request to Varro...."

I shook my head at the notion. "Apart from the fact that we will probably have to seek the former guest of a rich man among the free, unless fate has been very unkind to him, as punishment for his brutal deeds." That would have been right, after all, I thought.

"Anyway, he hasn't been able to torment another woman since then," Layla said grimly. "But you're right. He could be one of probably a dozen men at the ludus. Or someone from outside the school, who has enough money to buy a henchman on site, whom he subsequently killed when he was no longer in need of his services."

"You mean ... Rusticus?"

He had been a young lad, I would guess the same age as the gladiatrix. And only last night I'd looked at his undressed body in the medicus's hospital. Everything had still been in the right place between his legs, so Rusticus could not be the man who had once raped Nemesis and now wanted to blackmail her. But the hired villain of a wealthy backer—that would definitely have been a suitable role for the shady guard slave.

Layla nodded. "Isn't it obvious? Rusticus could move freely and unobtrusively within the ludus, and he liked to earn a little extra. What if the stranger whom Delia once mutilated offered him a large sum, enough money for Rusticus to buy his freedom and establish a comfortable existence? For such a bribe he would have been willing to commit murder, I'm sure."

"Just to be killed off inconspicuously himself after he'd done his duty, you mean."

"Exactly. When I went to Nemesis at noon today, I checked with the guards at the school beforehand. I wondered if any of them had seen Rusticus last night."

"And did they?" I asked. I should have come up with the idea of interrogating them myself.

"He left the ludus at a late hour, I was told. He was not on duty at the time. It was assumed he was going to a tavern to play dice, so no one was surprised."

"What if he was lured to the grave road on some pretext?" I pondered aloud. "If he really was the castrato's henchman, perhaps the latter promised him that he should now receive his just reward. In gold, in a place where no one was watching. And greedy as Rusticus was, he walked into a deadly trap."

"It may have been like that," Layla said.

"So that means that Delia's rapist is responsible for all the deaths that the ludus has had to mourn?" I summarized. "He committed the deeds in order to pin them on Nemesis—or rather, he instigated Rusticus to commit them. Because he wanted to bring the gladiatrix into the arena, as one condemned to death. When that didn't work, because we weren't convinced of her guilt, but instead started snooping around the school, that's when he changed his plan. He—that is, Rusticus, acting on his behalf—let loose the wild beasts in the ludus. Very close to Nemesis's chamber. But she survived again. The castrato then procured new henchmen, this band of robbers, but they screwed up their attack on the gladiatrix. They thought they had finished her off, but she wasn't dead yet."

"That would fit," Layla said, "though I still can't believe someone would go to such lengths. That he would kill people indiscriminately just to get his revenge on her."

I nodded. "But it also means that Nemesis is still in danger. This guy won't rest until he completes his work and she's dead."

"Optimus is aware of the danger," Layla said, "even if he doesn't know the background. He will protect Nemesis as long as she can't defend herself. No one can stop him from doing that, even if he ends up paying for his loyalty with a broken heart."

Layla grabbed my hand as we took the last steps back to the amphitheater. Only when we'd passed under the large round arches of the entrance area did she let go of it again. There was an expression of pain and anger on her beautiful dark face, but also of confusion.

XXXV

The fifth and last day of the games offered an extraordinary spectaculum once again. And this time I was even present to watch it for most of the day.

In the morning, a venator was almost torn to pieces by a huge tiger. The animal seemed voraciously hungry, and angry because of its long captivity. It pounced on the venator with its mighty paws, snarling, baring its razor-sharp teeth, driving the audience to veritable storms of excitement.

It fought so bravely, so majestically, that many spectators wished—and made this desire known with loud shouts—that this one time the beast might emerge victorious from the fight. The venator, however, kept the upper hand, even if he wasn't able to leave the arena upright afterwards. Atticus would have to do his best so that the man's career would not end here today.

Before the fights of the afternoon, the lottery that was so popular with the audience was held. *Sportulae*, small wooden balls, were thrown up to the tiers—and whoever caught them could redeem a prize. There was gold to be won, but also the meat of the magnificent tiger, a coveted delicacy, for example—plus memorabilia of the games. There were oil lamps and vessels depicting battle scenes, and clay figures of the most famous gladiators, including Nemesis. On the higher tiers, as happened so often during this part of the program, one or another tooth was knocked out and many a rib was broken in order to get hold of one of the coveted balls.

Among the fights of the afternoon, one spectaculum was worth mentioning, which I myself had never observed anywhere before: the duel of two gladiators of the particularly rare type, the *sagittarius.*

Archers! One can imagine that this battle was entirely different from the duels of the various melee fighters.

But I don't want to get lost in descriptions of the games; rather I prefer to continue reporting how we got on with the murder mystery. Although the honest answer to this question must be: not at all.

We continued to be stuck, feeling like we were running around in circles like well-mules. While Layla and I followed the fighting in the arena, we simultaneously speculated in whispers who the mysterious avenger might be who wanted to pay Nemesis back for his castration.

We juggled names back and forth, judged whether the men might be of the right age and whether they had fathered any children that we knew of—which would have been evidence that they were still in full possession of their manhood. We tried to trace where the possible suspects had been at the times of the various murders ... and so on and so forth. We simply could not succeed in settling on a promising culprit.

I indicated that the marriage of Iulianus and his wife had remained childless, that Petronella sought her erotic fulfillment in the arms of gladiators, and that her husband had urged Marcellus to execute the gladiatrix. "I think it's quite possible that Iulianus is our wanted man," I said to

Layla.

She, however, was not convinced. I think her suspicions centered mainly on the gladiators, specifically on those among them who had enrolled in the ludus of their own accord, or even roamed the empire completely independently, only letting themselves be hired from fight to fight.

As I said, we didn't get anywhere.

In the evening, when the games had come to an end with the final parade and the sacrifices to the gods, we returned to the ludus.

We encountered a sleepy Optimus, who had set up camp outside Nemesis's chamber, ready to defend her with his life, and bravely holding out there. We learned that Atticus had been intensively tending to the wounded gladiatrix during the day, and that she was already regaining some of her strength.

When we visited her in her chamber, her numerous bandages reminded me somewhat of a living mummy, but her spirit was already back to its old self: proud, stubborn and fierce. She swore revenge on the band of robbers who had ambushed her in so cowardly a fashion.

Yes, she stuck to her story. I didn't address her about her past, because I was far from convinced that this castrato she had told Layla about actually existed. I wondered if he really were hiding among the people at the ludus, or in the immediate periphery of the games. Layla, on the other hand, was dead certain that the gladiatrix had told her the truth and nothing but the truth.

Nemesis asked us when she could leave. I put her off by saying that she would have to stay at the school for another two or three days anyway, until she was strong enough for the rigors of a journey.

She was content with that for now.

For Marcellus, she was still the prime suspect as far as the murders at the ludus were concerned, but he had told me today on the VIP stand that he'd leave it to me—and Layla—to decide the fate of the gladiatrix.

In his view, the deaths at the school could remain unsolved forever. Now that the games were over, those bloody deeds would quickly be forgotten, at least in high society. Only gladiators, slaves, and convicted criminals had fallen victim to the murderer. No respected citizen of the city had been injured, and no one would complain if the legate did not look further into these crimes. After all, that was not his job.

According to Roman law, anyone who wanted to put a murderer on the cross had to take care of gathering evidence himself and then drag the guilty party before a court. Only when an attack was directed against the legion itself—or against an honorable citizen of the city—did the legate intervene. What happened in the ludus, a place of no reputation, was of course worth a little gossip, but in truth no one really cared.

Layla had vouched for Nemesis's innocence in the aforementioned conversation with Marcellus. She did not tell her lover anything about the gladiatrix's past—as she had sworn to her she would not—but the legate still trusted her word.

"As I've said," he repeated, "I place the fate of this woman in your hands. If you think she is innocent, let her go her way."

In other words, it had become clear that Marcellus did not want to deal with this vexed matter any longer.

When we were in the gladiator school that evening, I also had a discreet conversation with the medicus.

I asked Atticus if he might have perhaps noticed a wound in the genital area of one of the gladiators he had treated at the ludus. That is how I paraphrased it; I wanted to give him as few details as possible about exactly what kind of injury I was concerned with, and why I was looking for such a man.

Atticus was certainly not a talker who would spill the beans right away, but eventually every piece of news got around. Especially in a place like the school, where so many men lived together in a small space, and many of them—the slave-gladiators in particular—were excluded from all opportunities for entertainment on offer to a free man in a small town like Vindobona. They were left with only the gossip that permeated every wall, every cell door in the ludus.

Atticus, however, looked at me uncomprehendingly. No, he had not noticed any such injury. No self-respecting arena fighter aimed at the genitals of his opponent.

I knew that, of course, but I could not explain myself to Atticus. So I left the hospital without having achieved anything at all.

XXXVI

In the night I rolled sleeplessly in my bed. Marcellus might not care who was ultimately responsible for the murders in the ludus, but I wanted to know the truth! I would consider it a personal defeat if this murder case remained unsolved forever. I did not want to fail in my role of investigator which I had assigned myself so pridefully.

However, the next morning I was to forget all these ridiculous vanities in one fell swoop.

I had hardly awakened when—once again—a messenger at the gate was reported to me. I quickly dressed and directed my steps into the atrium, dreading news from Optimus that something had happened to Nemesis. Or perhaps another murder had taken place that cast doubt on the gladiatrix's innocence?

But when I saw the man standing in front of me, I realized that he was not from the school. He looked ragged, still bearing fresh wounds on his arms and face. When I stepped toward him, he looked at me as if he was about to burst into tears.

I had never seen this man before—or so I thought. But at second glance he seemed somehow familiar to me.

Only when he began to speak did I realize who he was: one of the servants Alma had traveled with before, last year, when I had met her on the tour to the Wonders of the World.

I could not remember his name, but I knew that he had been a strong and capable fellow. The man from my memory had hardly anything in common with the heap of misery that now stood in my atrium, looking at me as if I were his executioner.

"My mistress," he exclaimed, "she's been kidnapped!"

His voice broke—and I felt as if he had rammed a blade into my guts.

"What are you saying?" I stammered.

"We ... we were ambushed," he reported haltingly. "Not half a day's journey from here. Robbers ambushed us, killed most of the guards, stormed the wagon ... and carried Alma off. They spared her life, I think," he added quickly as he watched me slump down on a bench.

"And me as well, the only one of all the guards. As I now know, they spared me so that I could deliver their demands to you."

"Their *demands*? Do they want to extort gold for Alma's life?"

So there was hope! I was a wealthy man, my coffers well filled. No matter what sum they'd demanded for Alma's life, I would pay it! And save my beloved!

"They don't want gold from you," the fellow abruptly interrupted my thoughts. "They demand another woman in return for Alma's release."

"Another woman?" I repeated, uncomprehending.

"Her name is Nemesis. I was told you know her well. *It's her life for Alma's.* That's the message I'm supposed to give you."

He rattled off more details, mentioning a place I knew well: an abandoned homestead less than two miles west of my house, not far from the road that lined the north bank of the Danubius. It was where I must take the gladiatrix, today, at the fourth hour of the night.

"I have to emphasize that you must come alone," continued the messenger. "If the kidnappers were to see even one man in your company, Alma is as good as dead. It has to be only you and the gladiatrix. You will hand her over to them, and in return Alma will be released."

His eyes narrowed with concern. "You will save my mistress, Thanar? She's very fond of you, I'm sure you know that. You won't abandon her, will you?"

"Of course not," I snapped. What did this fellow think of me?

"Who are those men who kidnapped Alma?" I questioned him. "What can you tell me about them?"

The messenger shrugged and looked perplexed. "I thought they were plain old bandits when they attacked us. But such bastards would have demanded gold from you, wouldn't they? Who is this Nemesis, that they want to get hold of her so badly? Why didn't they kidnap her directly instead of taking Alma first?"

I could have provided him with some answers to his questions. For example, that they had already had Nemesis in their power, but had failed in her murder. She had escaped with her life, and now she was guarded around the clock.

"When was it that you were attacked?" I asked, turning to the fellow again.

"Three days ago, sir."

A groan escaped my throat. So I had been right to expect Alma in Vindobona long ago. She had almost reached the city—only to fall into the hands of these scoundrels. And Layla had once again shown the right instinct about our murder case.

Nemesis was innocent; I finally had proof. She was the victim, not the perpetrator. And now her enemy was openly demanding her head. I should deliver Nemesis to him, sacrifice her life in exchange for Alma's—if one could trust such a scoundrel at all, and his hostage was not already dead. But I didn't want to even think about that.

The fact that Alma had already been kidnapped three days ago also meant that whoever was after Nemesis's life had acted with foresight. Alma had been kidnapped even before the gladiatrix herself was ambushed. Nemesis's enemy—the castrato?—had hedged his bets, and devised a backup plan. In case his main strategy wouldn't work out.

"Where were they holding you?" I asked the messenger again.

He shook his head. "I don't know, sir. They put sacks over our heads when we were taken away. And even now I was left about half a mile north of your property with a blindfold on. I was told which way to go and how to find your house."

"And now that you've delivered the message...?"

"They told me to return to the same place, where they dropped me off, with your answer, Thanar. But you must not follow me, they drilled that into me! Otherwise they will execute Alma."

He hesitated for a moment. "*Or worse,*" he added then. "Those were the words of the leader."

"The leader? What does he look like, can you describe him?"

Once again hope rekindled in me, but again I was met with a shake of the head.

"I was blindfolded the whole time, sir. But I can tell you that he speaks like an educated man; not a common street thief, if you know what I mean."

I gasped for breath. My atrium spun around me—the sculptures I was so proud of, the rich wall paintings, the floor mosaic, and my weapons, axes, swords, and saxes, which adorned the walls—it all seemed to descend upon me as if they were animated by demonic forces.

I let my head sink into my hands, trying to catch my breath and shake off the paralysis.

"Tell them I will do as I am asked," I finally said to the messenger. "I will be on hand, tonight. With Nemesis at my side, as they demand."

XXXVII

No sooner had I dismissed the messenger than I had my fastest horse saddled and rode to the legate's palace.

Marcellus and Layla were lying together in one of the dining rooms and had just taken their breakfast. They must have seen the turmoil I was in, because Marcellus was immediately on his feet and rushing to meet me as soon as a slave had led me into the room.

I described to him—and to Layla—everything that had happened to me and finally let myself sink wearily onto one of the couches.

"Who even knew I was expecting Alma's arrival?" I said, to no one in particular.

Marcellus sat down by me and put one of his strong hands on my arm. "I'm afraid almost anyone, my friend."

I raised my eyebrows, looking at him uncomprehendingly.

"Haven't you noticed?" he said. "You've been talking of nothing else for the past few days and even weeks ... before the murders at the ludus captured your attention. Just think of the guest banquet on the eve of the games!"

I had to admit to myself that he was right.

That evening, I had actually mentioned to everyone I'd talked to that I was impatiently awaiting Alma's arrival, raving about her beauty, telling them about the trip to the Wonders of the World on which we had met, and much more. And that evening alone, in addition to the sponsors of the games, Varro and a good two dozen gladiators from the ludus had been present.

"The fact that you have been trying to find the murderer who is wreaking havoc in the ludus won't have escaped anyone's notice either," Marcellus added. "That has made you the target of this villain. He wants to take you out, to silence you, and at the same time he's lusting after the gladiatrix's head, whatever drives him to it. Alma is your Achilles heel, the perfect leverage to get you to act."

He gave Layla a look that didn't escape me.

I knew what he was thinking: Layla had investigated the murder cases at Varro's school with me, and she, too, was the object of my loyal affection, if no longer my lover. The kidnappers could just as well have grabbed Layla.

Alma had merely been the easier target. The bandits, for all their nefariousness, probably did not want to incur the wrath of the legate. And breaking into the legate's palace to steal Layla was an impossibility.

"What opponents should I expect, what do you think?" I asked my friends. "And how can I outsmart them? How can I save Alma's life without sacrificing that of Nemesis?"

I would certainly not act as these criminals had done and kidnap the gladiatrix, for my part. I knew that I'd condemn her to death with the exchange they had demanded of me.

"*We* will find a way to outsmart them," Marcellus replied. "You're not on your own—I hope I don't have to tell you that."

I nodded gratefully, but saw no way we could beat the villains without risking the lives of both Alma and Nemesis.

I couldn't seem to come up with any plan at all. All I could think of was that my Alma had been held captive by these fiends for days. I felt sick at the thought of what they might have done to her during that time.

"As for our opponents," Marcellus continued, "I think we should expect street bandits; a whole gang, probably. If Nemesis spoke the truth, she was ambushed by these scoundrels on the grave road, led by Brigantius, who escaped his execution. But not for long, I swear on my honor!"

Brigantius ... he could not be the one whom Nemesis had once castrated and who was now bent on revenge. His eyes were the wrong color.

But what if Nemesis was mistaken? Her memory could be deceptive after all these years.

"Someone must have hired Brigantius to kill Nemesis," I said. "That's why he and his gang ambushed Alma and kidnapped her."

Marcellus shook his head. "What demon is driving this thug to get involved in such an undertaking? It doesn't matter what sum he was offered for it, surely he must know with whom he is getting involved and what he is putting on the line! He has just escaped execution, by an incredible stroke of luck, a veritable act of Fortuna such as any man hardly experiences in his life ... and what does he do? Goes and again risks his neck! His client must be very wealthy and must have offered Brigantius an insane sum for his services. I can't explain it any other way."

"What if it wasn't an act of Fortuna at all?" Layla said, taking the floor.

"Excuse me?" Marcellus looked at her in irritation.

"That Brigantius escaped his execution, I mean. What if it was more than just a lucky coincidence?"

XXXVIII

When the fourth hour of the night had come, I was sitting on the coach box of one of the wagons that I normally used for transporting my goods.

It was a plain vehicle, pulled by two horses, and with an open loading area behind the coachman's bench. There I had stretched a tarpaulin, which was fastened with leather straps to the side boards of the wagon; a floating hospital stretcher on which we had bedded Nemesis.

The construction would soften the bumpy jolts of the ride a little and make a severely injured person's last journey a little more bearable. The gladiatrix lay motionless behind me, as if she were completely immobile due to her wounds, or even unconscious. I had wrapped her in a warm blanket, and not only to arm her against the chill of the night.

We had not tolerated anyone but the medicus in her chamber for the whole day, and my faithful Optimus had spread the rumor in the ludus that the gladiatrix's condition had deteriorated badly—that the wounds inflicted on her at the grave road would not heal and were draining her vitality.

My good Optimus! After brooding over a battle plan for tonight with Marcellus and Layla in the legate's palace, I had rushed to the ludus and taken my old friend into my confidence.

Optimus had immediately been ready to stand by me, but had also made it clear that he would defend Nemesis's life with his own. Exchanging her for Alma was out of the question for him.

I had expected nothing else, and of course I would never have demanded such a sacrifice.

The gladiatrix herself reacted with amazing calm to my explanations—and to what I had to ask from her. Namely, that she come with me voluntarily to the fateful meeting in the night.

She had tilted her head and given me a strangely melancholy look.

"I am impressed by such devotion from a man to a woman," she told me. "That you would willingly walk into an ambush to save Alma, who isn't even your wife, or the mother of your children; I myself have never had such a thing happen to me."

"What are you talking about?" I returned heatedly. "Optimus would do anything for you that your heart desires. And more! Don't you realize that?"

I could have sworn that an expression of gentleness flitted across her face that I had not seen there before. But in the next moment she was already under complete self-control again.

"I will come with you tonight," she said, "as a severely injured person in the back of your wagon, as you ask me to do."

As darkness fell, I drove up to the front of the ludus in the wagon I've already described, and a couple of sturdy slaves hauled Nemesis out of her chamber on a stretcher. I instructed the lads to lay her carefully down on the tarpaulin and to spread a blanket over her body against the cool night air.

Then we drove off, past the legionary camp and then over the bridge that spanned the Danubius. We passed my house.

And now I was on my way to the abandoned homestead that Alma's kidnappers had set as the meeting place for the exchange of the two women. I let the horses trot along at a leisurely pace so as not to cause any pain to the ostensibly severely-wounded woman I was transporting.

In truth, Nemesis had recovered amazingly fast from her injuries. Well, she was still pretty wobbly on her feet, and Atticus had put so many bandages on her that one really did think of a mummy when looking at her.

But her courage was unbroken. She seemed eager to finally meet her archenemy face to face, and to destroy once and for all this man who was behind Alma's abduction and the countless acts of bloodshed in the school.

It had been a long time since I myself had sat on the coach box of one of my wagons.

As I steered the horses along the riverside path, my mind wandered back to the early days of my career as a trader.

At that time, I had not been squeamish about the origin of my goods, and I had traveled throughout the country myself, on a wagon very similar to the one I was driving tonight. Back then, I had not been able to afford guards, or men to make these arduous journeys on my behalf. So

I had fallen victim to brigands more than once. I could count myself lucky that I was still alive and that the gods had blessed my business with rich profits.

I straightened myself on the carriage seat, looked around, and pricked up my ears. Now was really not the time for sentimental thoughts of the past, even if I would have preferred to be anywhere tonight but on this road.

It was deserted at this late hour. Only the sounds of various animals came from the forest, which crept up close to the path and the riverbank and seemed to extend to the northern end of the world.

I listened, trying to hear the howling of a pack of wolves, but without success. The light of the moon glittered silver on the waters of the Danubius.

I had not brought a lamp, preferring to find my way under cover of darkness. I knew this river bank, and the place I was heading for, very well.

Another thought forced itself into my head, Layla's words this morning in the legate's palace: what if Brigantius didn't survive the poison attack on the convicts by a mere stroke of luck?

Both Marcellus and I had not understood at first what she was getting at with this strange statement.

"What if the attack on the condemned was in fact not an experiment to test the assassin's poison for the perfect dose," she'd continued, "but a very deliberate diversion to free Brigantius?"

Six men had actually been poisoned, but a seventh—Brigantius—had perhaps only received a strong sleeping draught to put him into a death-like state. This deception would not have withstood a thorough examination by a medicus, but with seven supposed corpses and in the midst of ongoing games in the arena, there had been no time to take a closer look.

Rusticus, the hired helper at the ludus, had made sure that Brigantius was taken to the corpse shed together with the actual dead. The following night he'd opened the door for him and helped him to escape from the school.

The murderer had then tried to blame his mass killing of the convicts—just like the murder of the two gladiators Mevia and Nicanor—on the gladiatrix, to bring her to the cross for it. Or to have her die *ad bestias* in the arena.

That was Layla's new theory, which she had presented to us with great passion. She was convinced that she was right.

"The killer had *two* goals, you know," she pointed out, "not just one. I think he wanted to save Brigantius and destroy Nemesis at the same time."

"Which he almost succeeded in doing," Marcellus added with a scowl. He himself would probably have had Nemesis executed if Layla had not vouched for the gladiatrix's innocence.

Layla continued: "Brigantius then ambushed Nemesis in return for the patron who'd made his escape possible, almost killing the gladiatrix on the grave road. But there he committed a fatal mistake, by not ensuring her demise before leaving her. Perhaps travelers on the southern road got in the way, and he and his men had to quickly run for the hills."

If the robber chief had not been so sloppy, the gladiatrix would be dead now. We would never have known a word about the man whom she had castrated and who'd sworn revenge for Baiae in his letter to her.

Nemesis would have been blamed post mortem for the murders at the ludus, and we would not have investigated further. Case closed.

But wait, that was not quite true. Alma was already in the hands of her kidnappers at that point. Would they have simply executed her, and thus I'd never have heard how and why she had disappeared? The thought made my chest even tighter than it already was.

I gave the horses some rein, clicking my tongue to spur them on. I still had a lot of time before the appointed hour, but now I was eager to get the meeting over with, however it might end.

XXXIX

When I reached the abandoned homestead where the exchange was to take place, I was amazed at how dilapidated it truly was.

The roof had long since collapsed, and the remains of the stone walls were overgrown by moss and vines. I had not passed by here for a long time, and why should I? Ruins like these belonged to the creatures of the forest; we humans had no interest in them anymore. Only shady riffraff like Brigantius and his henchmen prowled around in such places.

I waited seemingly an endless amount of time.

Then, finally, a single man showed himself. He stepped out from between a few trees that lined the small clearing. At first he was no more than a shadow in the darkness, coming to within ten or fifteen paces, then stopping.

I could see nothing of his face. He was dressed in a dark cloak with a hood, and either he was a Nubian like Layla or he had blackened his face with soot. I felt like I was staring into an abyss as I tried to make out his features.

When he finally addressed me, I recognized the man's voice: it was Brigantius!

We had interrogated him for hours after we'd caught him; he hadn't talked much, but enough that his voice was memorable to me.

He hadn't revealed the names of his gang members, or

where their hideouts and the caches of their rich booty were located, even under torture. We'd had no choice but to be satisfied with his capture and to make his death in the arena a spectacle for the people who had suffered for so long under the attacks of his gang.

I had hoped that his remaining men would scatter without their leader, that they would seek their fortune in other parts of the empire and join gangs that were up to mischief far from Vindobona.

But now Brigantius stood before me again—alive—free— and with Alma in his power.

I addressed him by his name so that he should know that I had recognized him.

"Brigantius, I'm bringing you the gladiatrix just as you've asked." I pointed with my thumb over my shoulder to the loading area of the wagon, where Nemesis lay motionless on the stretched tarpaulin.

Brigantius looked around, then silently approached me.

I was sure that he had not come alone; some of his men were definitely lurking in the dense forest that surrounded us. The only question was: how many?

He wanted to climb on the wagon and reach for Nemesis, but I jumped off the carriage stand and blocked him.

"Stop!" I exclaimed. "First I want to see Alma. Prove to me that she is well."

"You seriously think you can make demands?" he replied with a sneer. "A truly brave barbarian you are, I must say. But also a fool, to risk your life for a woman!"

He had not pulled the hood from his hair when I'd called his name. But now he lifted his head without hesitation, so that I could make out his blue eyes in the black-painted face. It was him without a doubt.

I held my ground, stood up to him, and prevented him from getting any closer to Nemesis. Instead I let him see the pommel of my short sword, which I wore on my belt under my cloak, and I reiterated my demand.

"Bring me Alma and the gladiatrix will be yours, just as we agreed. Or is your word worth nothing?"

He didn't let this insult stand. "Ha! You shall have your beautiful sweetheart back," he promised me, in a mockingly gallant tone.

He peered at the load area of my wagon. "But first I want to make sure you're not a cheat, trying to offer me some half-dead whore instead of the gladiatrix! Let me see her face."

I let him have his way. He narrowed his eyes and studied the features of the motionless woman for a moment.

Then he turned, barking an order toward the edge of the forest: "Bring in the barbarian's bitch!"

The words cut into my heart. I had to muster all my self-control not to slam my fist into the bandit leader's face.

Two villains, also in hooded cloaks, emerged out of the darkness and came toward us. Between them they led a brightly dressed figure who had been blindfolded. Alma!

Behind them, a third brigand left the shelter of the trees. He quickened his steps so that he arrived at my wagon at the same time as the others.

His face was also blackened with soot, his figure hidden under a cloak. It was impossible to see anything for sure in the moonlight, but I still had the impression that his garment was of finer quality, and not the kind of rags that common street thieves usually wrapped themselves in.

Who was this man? The castrato, Nemesis's arch enemy? The true leader of these robbers, or at any rate their client in recent weeks?

My gaze hurried from him to Alma, over her face, her arms, and what could be seen of her legs under the long tunic in which she was robed.

She looked unharmed, but still I didn't dare imagine what these bandits might have done to her. I would have loved to draw my sword and massacre these scoundrels with my own hands.

But I restrained my rage. I was not a gladiator, not even a particularly daring fighter, though I knew how to handle a sword or an axe. I could not take on these four enemies alone.

I stretched out my arms toward Alma to signal the bandits to release her. But that would probably have been too easy.

The two villains flanking her would not let her go. They didn't even take off her blindfold.

So all I could do was direct a few brief words to my beloved, to assure her that I was with her. That she was safe, that everything would be all right soon.

Brigantius burst out laughing. "You are an amusing fellow, Thanar!" he barked.

At that moment, the man who until now had remained in the background intervened—the better-dressed man, in whom I suspected the castrato.

"Get the gladiatrix off the wagon," he ordered me, "then you can have your bitch."

He took a step towards me, so close that his breath hit me in the face, but all the while looking past me and hiding his own face from me while he addressed me directly. He did not want to be recognized, that was quite clear.

"You'll have to take the wagon with you if you want to get the gladiatrix away from here alive," I told the man, while at the same time racking my brain, trying to identify him by the few words he'd uttered. He'd spoken in good Latin, like an educated man, and he seemed somehow familiar. But I couldn't place his voice with any certainty, no matter how hard I tried. It seemed to me that he was deliberately disguising it.

"The wagon?" he repeated. His words were full of cold anger, full of hatred for the gladiatrix he was finally going to get his hands on. He had to be the castrato!

"She's badly injured," I replied. "Do you just want to take her dead body with you? Or do you want her to arrive alive—wherever you want to take her? Then use the wagon. You can have it."

"How generous of you," he sneered.

"You can do whatever you're going to do with her right here, as well, if you'd rather," I added. "Her fate means nothing to me; she is doomed to die anyway. She has a day or two left at the most, so badly did your henchmen wound her."

Again I stretched out my arms, and this time the castrato signaled with his head to the two villains holding Alma. The men let her go, one of them tearing the bandage from her eyes.

She blinked for a moment, then stumbled toward me with a low moan. I pulled her to me, pressed her trembling body tightly against mine and gave way to the castrato.

I saw a dagger flash in the man's hand as he prepared to climb into the back of my wagon.

"I had hoped for a longer-lasting pleasure," I heard him say, "to inflict greater torment on this witch now that she is finally mine. But I *will* make her suffer quite a bit, before she takes refuge in death. And rest assured, barbarian, that later on every one of my men will desecrate her corpse!"

As vile as this threat was, it instilled in me the certainty that this man was indeed the bastard that Nemesis had once castrated. Otherwise he probably would not have missed the opportunity to desecrate her corpse himself, but he was no longer able to do so, because his manhood had fallen victim to Nemesis's teeth.

He bent over the side wall of my wagon, wanting to reach for the gladiatrix's hair and plunge the blade into her throat. "For Baiae!" I heard him growl.

But Nemesis, nowhere near as close to death as I had claimed, tore the blanket from her body at that moment and parried his attack with the sword she had kept hidden beneath it.

Quickly I pushed Alma behind me, drew my own weapon and faced the men who immediately rushed to the castrato's aid.

Nemesis was not strong enough to attack boldly or even jump off the wagon. But with her sword, she was at least able to stop her attacker from finishing her off on the spot. And no sooner had he recovered from this surprise than the tarpaulin, stretching out beneath Nemesis's body, suddenly began to shift.

The suspensions of the fabric on the edge of the wagon came loose as if by magic.

Two men jumped up, who had been hiding under the tarp. Two friends to whom I would have entrusted my life, and in whose hands Alma's fate now lay. And that of Nemesis. That was the real reason why we had put the tarp on the wagon in the first place: to hide the two of them under it.

Marcellus and Optimus.

You must come alone, the messenger of the bandits had impressed upon me. But my friends had not abandoned me.

With wild fury and swift blades, Optimus and the legate attacked our enemies. I joined them, and the three of us pounced on the four brigands.

The castrato was faster than I would have thought possible. He had jumped from the wagon at the very moment when my two friends had appeared from under the tarpaulin. The two lads who had brought Alma had rushed stout-heartedly to his side, indeed, had pushed themselves protectively in front of him. Now the two of them fought Optimus and Marcellus, while I rushed at Brigantius.

We had to keep an eye on the castrato! He might be armed only with a dagger, but a deft side blow, delivered against one of us, could seal our fate just as well as a direct sword thrust from our opponents.

However, he did not think to enter the fray with his tiny blade. Instead he brought his thumb and forefinger to his lips and let out a shrill whistle.

I had a bad feeling—and immediately afterwards my worst fears were confirmed.

Behind the villains, the forest suddenly seemed to come to life. However it was not tree trunks that had started to move, but a whole crowd of men who were jumping out from under the branches. Brigantius's band, rushing to the aid of their captain. I counted seven men, then ten, twelve....

I gave up counting.

I sent up a whispered prayer to the gods.

Above my head, in a treetop near the clearing, an owl hooted. I barely heard it, so violently was my pulse pounding in my temples.

The bandits came at us, silently and quickly, sword blades and axes glittering in the moonlight. The castrato and the three men we had just been fighting beat a hasty retreat. Marcellus and Optimus, accomplished warriors as they were, would have defeated them in no time, and I myself had at least been able to hold my own against Brigantius.

But to go up against the almost two dozen villains who were now coming at us would be beyond even the heroism and strength of my intrepid friends.

XL

I heard the wolves before I saw them. The wind carried their howls through the forest, just before Brigantius's henchmen could close their circle around us.

Marcellus and Optimus let the two villains they had been fighting go and held their ground. Brigantius struck at me one more time with his sword, but missed, and then joined his men. They kept their distance from us and formed a united front with their reinforcements, who had been waiting for this moment in the shelter of the trees.

Brigantius was no fool. He had to have expected that I would try a ruse. He had prepared himself for this eventuality with a horde of armed men.

But he had not expected a pack of angry wolves—or rather, two or three packs! As the bandits had done just before, it was now the hairy bodies of the beasts that emerged from the darkness of the forest. I counted about twenty animals in a flash, because they moved faster than my eyes could track them.

The wolves rushed at the bandits from behind, like an unleashed tidal wave of muscular bodies and belligerently bared teeth. Their howls were deafening. Even at twenty paces away, I thought I could feel their hot breath, sense it on my skin, smell its ghastly stench.

Fiercer than any cavalry, the beasts attacked, leaving the bandits no time to pounce on us or even to snatch Alma or Nemesis from our grasp.

The brigands were surprised, scared to death by this attack—but my friends and I were not.

We made sure to put a healthy distance between us and the scoundrels, who now had to turn around to face the bloodthirsty wolves at their backs. The villains might have expected human attackers, but not a pack of wild beasts.

I grabbed Alma and lifted her with a powerful swing onto the back of my wagon, where Nemesis reached out and pulled her up.

Optimus and Marcellus reined in the horses, which were rearing up with loud whinnies. With quick hands they loosened the harness that held the two steeds in front of the wagon. The animals had been in mortal fear since the wolves had stormed into the clearing.

We let the horses flee. It was impossible to turn the wagon with such frightened draft animals in the tiny clearing. I was ready to sacrifice the horses if they could not escape the wolves, even though I would have felt sadness for the faithful animals.

But the wolf pack had already found plenty of food anyway, and it was much slower on its feet than any horse.

My friends and I, though, didn't try to escape, because behind us further dark shadows were now appearing. This time, however, they were not robbers, but allies. They were some battle-hardened guards who were in my service—as well as a handful of legionaries whom Marcellus had selected.

They had followed my wagon at a great distance, creeping through the forest one by one, so as not to be discovered and thereby endanger Alma's life. But now that the bandits were busy with the wolves, and Alma sat safely behind me in the wagon, they could go on the attack.

What can I say? They made short work of any villains who had escaped the wolves.

And as far as the beasts were concerned, it was not a benevolent god who had sent them to us at just the right moment, but rather a man who knew like no other how to catch such animals, how to direct them to where he wanted them and to ignite their anger in a wild fight. Faustinius, my faithful friend the animal trader.

We were victorious, no—triumphant!

After the wolves had swept over the bandits like an army of vengeful furies, my guards and Marcellus's soldiers took on the survivors.

A few of the wolves naturally attacked our men, but fortunately they were prepared for such an attack. They had protected their arms and legs with those well-padded bandages that were also used by certain types of gladiators. In addition, they received support from Faustinius and his men, who quickly chased away the remaining beasts.

In the end, the clearing was stained red with the blood of the bandits. A dozen or so of the villains lay dead on the forest floor with bitten limbs, while the survivors were rounded up by our men, incapacitated and put in shackles.

Brigantius was among the dead. He was only recognizable by his bright blue eyes, which gazed at us in a broken stare. The rest of his face had turned into a squashed red mass.

The leader, however, whom I've called the castrato, had survived. One of Marcellus's legionaries now dragged him to crouch at our feet. The fiend could barely walk under his own power, though he had spinelessly dug in behind his henchmen during the onslaught of the wolves. It had done him no good; the brave legionary had brought him down and ensured that he could not escape.

The hood still hung askew on his head as he knelt before us in the dust. He pulled it down himself, groaning as he got to his feet, and actually had the guts to stick his chin out when we looked him in the eye.

And who was he, this nefarious killer who had brought so much suffering to the ludus of Vindobona?

Cornix! The oh-so-honorable merchant who had hosted the gladiator games together with Marcellus and Iulianus.

I could not believe it. This respected citizen of Vindobona had been in league with a gang of robbers? And he was supposed to be the man who had once raped young Nemesis—and had been castrated by her for it?

Marcellus ordered his men to take him to the dungeon of the legionary camp, where we planned to extract from him everything that was still beyond our understanding. And we would certainly not be gentle in the process.

XLI

Two days after the events of that night, I had dinner with my friends. I'd invited them to my house and was entertaining them in the room that I jokingly called my barbarian lounge. Here, one did not lie at table on sofas, as the Romans used to do, but sat on benches and chairs with one's fellows around a large oaken table.

Alma was at my side, smiling, chatting cheerfully with me, eager to learn everything she didn't already know about the murders at the ludus.

She wore a dark red robe of fine cloth that Layla had given her as a gift. Her own robes had been stolen, along with the rest of her luggage, during the bandits' raid. She wore her hair braided into small pigtails draped on the back of her head, and her ears were adorned with two golden pendants that I had gifted her.

Never would an outsider have suspected that this woman had been freed from the captivity of vile brigands only a few days ago. Until this morning, she had kept to her bed and been only a little fevered. During the nights she had been haunted by nightmares. But now she seemed to be back to her old self; Alma was a real heroine.

To my left sat Layla and Marcellus, and on the opposite side of the table Optimus and Nemesis had taken their seats. They had been guests under my roof since the bloody battle in the forest.

And then, of course, there was Faustinius. He was sitting at the lower end of the table and was being served a cup of wine by one of my slaves. When he felt my gaze resting on him, he raised his head and toasted me.

I was infinitely happy to have all my friends safe and sound under my roof, while Cornix and the remaining members of Brigantius's band of bandits were incarcerated in the dungeon of the legionary camp, facing execution.

What none of us had suspected was that Cornix and Brigantius were brothers. Yes, the rich and respected citizen of Vindobona and the nefarious robber chief.

Who would have ever thought it? Cornix had confessed it to us when we interrogated him. That and much more. His eyes were full of hate as we forced the truth out of him. But he knew that his fate was sealed and owned up to all his misdeeds without Marcellus having to torture him first.

So Brigantius and Cornix, what a mismatched team!

Each of them went about his own business, but nevertheless they were bound to each other by an unbreakable loyalty. To some extent, Cornix also acted as a fence for the stolen goods that Brigantius captured on his raids. He sold valuable jewelry and the like through his trading network to distant Rome, where no one asked about the origin of the jewels.

When Brigantius was imprisoned and threatened with execution, Cornix had devised a plan to save his brother. He'd acted as co-sponsor of the games in which Brigantius was to meet his end in the arena. This had given him access to the ludus, and he'd been able to look around among the guards there for a man suitable to his purposes. Someone who'd be willing to do whatever Cornix told him to for the appropriate sum.

He'd found this man, who was greedy for gold and had no conscience, in Rusticus. He'd promised the fellow such a handsome sum that he could buy himself free of Varro and build a carefree existence.

But at the school Cornix had also made the acquaintance of Nemesis, the famous gladiatrix who was to be one of the main attractions of the games. He recognized in her—not least thanks to the fiery mark on her neck—the young woman he had raped many years before in the house of a friend in Baiae, who had then mutilated him forever with her teeth.

This fateful meeting had changed Cornix's plans. Now it was not only a matter of saving his own brother from death; no, Cornix also thirsted for revenge against Nemesis. And so he'd instigated Rusticus, his hand in the ludus, in the commission of several murders. The two gladiators Nemesis was competing against in the arena were to die a suspicious death in order to stamp her as a murderer. A handful of convicts were sacrificed as well—not only to confirm suspicions against the gladiatrix, but more importantly in order to save Brigantius from the ludus in this way: he was to be taken to the corpse shed by Rusticus as a pseudo-corpse and then freed from the gladiatorial school late at night through a side gate.

So the poisoning of the convicts had not been an experiment, not a sideshow, but rather a means to the end Cornix was really after: to free Brigantius, and to do it in such a way that no one would chase him anymore, because he would be believed to be dead. This admittedly ingenious plan went wrong, however, when we noticed the disappearance of his body.

That Cornix had had the audacity to rob his victims of their teeth as well, in order to turn them into money, only showed how ice-cold and rapacious this man was, who had hidden himself so credibly behind the façade of a respectable citizen.

But Cornix's plan to vilify the gladiatrix as a murderer had not worked out. He hadn't succeeded in making her pay for the crimes that Rusticus had committed on Cornix's behalf. We had sought out the ludus that evening, at first even accompanied by Marcellus, but the gladiatrix had not been arrested. She'd remained unscathed, and we'd departed again.

Rusticus must have observed this and probably immediately sent a messenger to his master—or unobtrusively left the school late at night and made a report himself?

However, Cornix had had to come up with a new strategy to get back at the gladiatrix. He'd instructed his henchman to free the beasts in the ludus from their cages and sic them on Nemesis. Afterwards, Rusticus claimed that the gladiatrix had bewitched him and the other guards and was herself responsible for the animals' release. Another attempt to finally convince us of her guilt.

When this also failed, Cornix wrote a letter to his hated enemy in which he referred to the long-ago events of Baiae, thus luring Nemesis into an ambush. He must have been truly desperate to see the woman who'd once maimed him finally dead.

He'd also sent a message to Rusticus to meet him at the

same place—on the grave road south of the city. There the faithful henchman was to receive his promised payment. Instead, he'd found death at the hands of Brigantius's bandits, who—now free again—had thanked his brother in this way for saving him. Rusticus had done his duty and was no longer needed; now he was only a burden, an accessory, whom Cornix did not want to pay, but rather to get rid of once and for all.

Nemesis had also been overpowered by Brigantius and his bandits and left for dead.

Cornix himself could not be present at this raid. He had deliberately dined with his co-sponsors that evening—under my roof, of all places!—in order to secure a perfect alibi. Not that we even suspected him of being the mastermind behind the murders; both Layla and I had failed in this regard.

Cornix was a foresighted man. When he realized that slandering the gladiatrix was not going to work, he acquired a hostage that he could use in the worst case, should all his other plans fail—Alma. He had learned from me, silly blabbermouth that I was, that I was expecting her arrival in Vindobona any day now, and his brother had just needed to lie in wait for her with his bandits before she could reach the city.

Then, after Brigantius had been so sloppy in killing the gladiatrix, and the attempt to frame her for the murder of Rusticus had also failed, the time had come to send me a messenger and to offer an exchange. Alma's life for that of Nemesis.

Now that we were sitting together at dinner, I also told Alma what we had found out in the meantime about Cornix's past.

"His father, uncle and grandfather were already well-traveled merchants," I told her, "and it was at a friend of his grandfather's villa where Cornix stayed as a guest. That fateful summer in Baiae, when he met the young Nemesis. She was a slave in the host's house and..."

I bit my tongue. What was I doing? I was about to divulge the secret that Nemesis had entrusted to Layla under the seal of utmost secrecy!

I cleared my throat in embarrassment. Then I concluded my report with the following words: "Now let us say that the man did violence to her and she took bitter revenge on him."

Alma seemed to understand why I had come so abruptly to the end of my report.

She suddenly smiled and said, "Nemesis has already told me the story herself. Now that Cornix is doomed to die, she has made her peace with the past, I think. But still, we must be careful to keep her secret safe with us. She is, despite everything, a runaway slave, isn't she?"

I nodded wordlessly.

XLII

Next, Alma asked me to tell her about the plan we had made to rescue her from the bandits.

I bowed to her wishes.

"It was Layla who came up with the idea of the special wagon for the supposedly severely-wounded Nemesis. She herself directed some skilled slave girls in my house, who made the tarp with the leather suspensions in a few hours. Marcellus, who was quite the strategist, had insisted that we had to come up with a backup plan, in case his and Optimus's fighting strength would not be enough to defeat the villains. 'You never know how many men they'll have against us,' he said."

"Then *he* devised the plan with the wolves?" asked Alma. "I have never seen more ferocious beasts than those!"

I saw her tremble as if a shiver had run down her spine.

"The wolves were my idea," I said, with due modesty. "The element of surprise was to be on our side. It's also something Marcellus likes to talk about when he wants to entertain us yet again with military discussions at a guest banquet. And that day I remembered his words." I rolled my eyes theatrically.

Alma laughed, and that did me good.

"I can't believe how quickly Faustinius and his men managed to capture so many wolves," she said.

"Oh, there were a few left over from the games—some

particularly hungry specimens. And on top of that, Faustinius is an old hand when it comes to capturing beasts. Wolves are a piece of cake for him. He also takes on lions, bears, leopards, and even crocodiles or monster snakes."

Alma nodded. With thoughtful hand movements, she smoothed out the folds of her robe. The crimson really did go well with her fair skin and blond hair.

"I speculated that none of Brigantius's men would suspect anything," I continued, "even if they happened to run into the beast hunters that day in the forest. The idea that these wolves were being hunted at my request, to be used as weapons against my enemies in the evening, fortunately did not occur to them. Faustinius took care to transport the cages to a spot far from the meeting point agreed upon for the night, a good mile away from it in fact. And he was already there in the early evening hours to set out the cages. Having the cages in the woods would probably not have attracted any attention, even if one of the bandits had happened to discover them. Animal hunters often leave their captured beasts behind for a while until they can take them all away in the proper wagons."

Alma nodded again with an admiring expression in her eyes.

I liked that she wanted to know every detail of the unusual rescue operation. While I was telling the story, I kept looking for signs in her expression, her look, her posture, that she was really as well as she seemed to be.

To my great relief, I could discover nothing that would have made me doubt it. There was only one thing she hadn't done so far—and perhaps never would: she didn't say a word about the days of her imprisonment, told me absolutely nothing about what the villains had done to her. That was behind her now, she said, and she never wanted to think back to that time.

Of course, I respected her wishes and did not ask her further, but still I wondered if my company was good and healthy for her.

I had made it my vocation to hunt down criminals and solve murders. Could I in good conscience ask Alma to stay by my side? She made me vulnerable, and she would risk her life if she wanted to be my companion. Could I really put her through that? Or did I have to condemn myself to eternal loneliness?

I had asked Layla this question only yesterday, when we'd been able to have a conversation in private, while Alma was still lying in bed and had Nemesis to keep her company. She was particularly fond of the gladiatrix; Alma couldn't seem to get enough of her stories.

"Whether Alma wants to take the risk of being with you," Layla said, "is not for you to determine, Thanar. She has to decide that for herself, and I think she already has."

I had been satisfied with that, and now I remembered it with determination, driving away the gloomy thoughts and continuing with my report.

"So Faustinius and his hunters lay in wait, far enough from the meeting place so as not to be discovered. Only one of them climbed a giant tree that stood very close to the clearing. That, too, happened hours before the agreed-upon handover, so none of the bandits were roaming around there yet. They did show up some time before the appointed hour to secure the terrain, search the immediate area and post guards there, making sure that a dozen legionaries wouldn't be waiting for them at the appointed time. All this was observed by the scout from his tree. He too is an experienced man who knows his job. If you want to catch wild animals alive, good scouts are indispensable."

"*He* was the owl we heard?" asked Alma. "The one that screamed over our heads just after Brigantius mobilized his reinforcements?"

"Exactly. When the bandits came rushing out of the forest, he gave the agreed-upon signal. The call of an owl, which is not native here in the north, as Faustinius told me later. I must confess that I would not have noticed, but I am also not a man of the forest," I added with a smile.

"An unmistakable signal, then," Alma said. "And thereupon the hunters let the wolves out of the cages. And drove them toward the clearing."

"That's how it was. With torches and sticks they drove the wolves before them, irritated them, frightened them, which plunged the beasts into a furious rage. Faster than any rider, the animals covered the distance that led to the clearing—and there became our four-legged soldiers, slaughtering our opponents. They helped us to achieve a victory in which not a single one of our allies had to lay down his life."

I had made a rich sacrifice to the gods for such an outcome of our fight. I had been ready to risk my own life for Alma, but I would never have forgiven myself if something had happened to one of my friends—or my guards, or those legionaries who had followed their legate into this unusual battle.

Only a few wolves had met their deaths. Over the last days—as well as today—the meat of these brave beasts had found its way into my kitchen and thus to our evening table. We ate it as one used to eat the meat of wild animals after glorious animal fights in the arena, with praises to the gods and in the knowledge that the courage that these creatures had shown in life would pass on after their deaths to those who ate them.

Nemesis had begged the legate to allow her to take Cornix's life in a duel in the arena.

But Marcellus had preferred to make an example of the man. Every murderer, every street robber should think twice in the future before he pursued his dark plans in or around Vindobona.

Although Cornix was a respected citizen of our town, he was denied a merciful death by the sword. Instead, he was to be impaled—together with his surviving bandits—at a busy intersection on the Limes road.

Their corpses would be left there to rot for several weeks until the carrion birds had picked all the flesh from their bones. Only then would their remains be removed and dumped in the Danubius. An honorable grave was denied to criminals.

I glanced over at Optimus, who was engaged in an animated conversation with Nemesis. Judging by the few words I could catch, despite the babble of voices around the table, he was recounting episodes from his years of service in the legion.

I wondered what the future might hold for the two of them. Would there be a happy ending for the gladiatrix and the veteran legionary?

I think neither was yet ready to answer this question. For now, I had invited them to stay—for as long as they wanted to—as guests of my house.

I had compensated Varro, the lanista, for the temporary loss of his chief guard with a generous sum. In return, he had been quite gracious in conceding to a lower purchase price for Telephus. The axe fighter, whose eyesight was failing, now stood in my service.

I felt that after these gladiatorial games in Vindobona, so terribly eventful, we all deserved a break. And if the gods were kind to us, they would take their time before the next corpse fell at Layla's or my own feet.

Dramatis personae

Thanar: Germanic merchant with a weakness for Roman lifestyle & culture.
Layla: Thanar's freed slave and former lover, from the legendary kingdom of Nubia. Passionate sleuth & mystery solver.

Titus Granius Marcellus: legate (commander) of the legionary camp of Vindobona. Layla's lover. Main sponsor of the gladiatorial games.

Alma Philonica: a young widow from Rome, Thanar's love interest
Faustinius: animal trader. An old friend of Thanar's.

CO-SPONSORS OF THE GLADIATOR GAMES:

Cornix: wealthy trader
Aurelius Iulianus: new rich dentist
Petronella: his wife

GLADIATORS:

Nemesis: a free gladiatrix
Mevia: a still-inexperienced murmillo (heavy swordsman), condemned *ad gladius*
Nicanor: experienced free gladiator, thraex (medium

heavy fighter)

Telephus: experienced slave gladiator, axe fighter

Hilarius: free retiarius (net fighter)

OTHER PEOPLE IN THE LUDUS (GLADIATOR SCHOOL) OF VINDOBONA:

Varro: lanista (owner) of the ludus

Optimus: chief guard at the gladiator school. A former legionary and Thanar's friend.

Rusticus: a guard slave in the ludus

Atticus: medicus of the school

Brigantius: a robber chieftain sentenced to death

More from Thanar and Layla:

CURSED TO DIE
Murder in Antiquity, Book 5

A new murderer is wreaking havoc in the supposedly tranquil town of Vindobona.

The Germanic merchant Thanar, haunted again and again by terrible murder cases and meanwhile matured into an experienced private sleuth, has to face an unsolvable and very personal problem: his lover Alma has been suffering from terrible nightmares since her recent kidnapping by a murderous gang of robbers. She can no longer sleep, is wasting away, and even the best doctors in Vindobona can't seem to help her. Thanar's last hope is a witch, famous for her healing spells. But those who are able to save lives may also be willing to bring death....

More from Alex Wagner:

If you enjoyed *The Deadly Gladiatrix*, why not try my contemporary mystery series, too?—*Penny Küfer Investigates*—cozy crime novels full of old world charm.

About the author

Alex Wagner lives with her husband and 'partner in crime' near Vienna, Austria. From her writing chair she has a view of an old ruined castle, which helps her to dream up the most devious murder plots.

Alex writes historical as well as contemporary murder mysteries, always trying to give you sleepless nights. ;)

You can learn more about her and her books on the internet and on Facebook:

www.alexwagner.at
www.facebook.com/AlexWagnerMysteryWriter

Cover design: Estella Vukovic
Editor: Tarryn Thomas

Made in the USA
Las Vegas, NV
01 March 2024

86570847R00142